"I want a baby, Dane."

He tried to control his reaction. But Lacey saw his spine stiffen, his eyes widen the merest fraction. He looked as though he was about to speak. But he didn't.

"It's an overwhelming idea, I know."

"Overwhelming." Dane's eyes were clouded with a myriad of thoughts and emotions. "Lacey, let me get this straight. You're asking me—"

"To father my child."

"Why me?"

"Because you're perfect." She left it at that, then whispered, "You're also my last chance."

Donna Clayton is the recipient of the Diamond Author Award for Literary Achievement, as well as two Holt Medallions. As a child, she marvelled at the ability to travel the world, experience swashbuckling adventures and meet amazingly bold and daring people without ever leaving the shade of the huge oak tree in her garden. In her opinion, love *is* what makes the world go around.

One of her favourite pastimes is travelling. Her other interests include walking, reading, visiting friends, teaching Sunday school, cooking and baking, and she still collects cookbooks, too. In fact her house is overrun with them!

Recent titles by the same author:

HIS WILD YOUNG BRIDE
ADOPTED DAD
THE BOSS AND THE BEAUTY

WHO WILL FATHER
MY BABY?

BY
DONNA CLAYTON

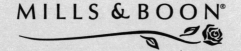
MILLS & BOON®

Much appreciation to
Joe and Bobbi McMullen of Wakefield Angus.
Thanks for patiently answering my questions!

*All the characters in this book have no existence outside the imagination
of the author, and have no relation whatsoever to anyone bearing the
same name or names. They are not even distantly inspired by any
individual known or unknown to the author, and all the incidents are
pure invention.*

*First published in Great Britain 2002
Harlequin Mills & Boon Limited,
Eton House, 18-24 Paradise Road, Richmond, Surrey TW9 1SR*

© Donna Fasano 2001

ISBN 0 263 83003 9

*Set in Times Roman 10½ on 12 pt.
02-0402-43919*

*Printed and bound in Spain
by Litografia Rosés, S.A., Barcelona*

Prologue

"**W**hat is it with men and their sperm?" Lacy Rivers sorted through the mail, but she was so distracted that she was going through the morning ritual purely by rote. "Suggest a night of frivolous fun and a man will jump your bones without a second thought. But you just mention the word *baby* and he acts as if his bodily fluids are more precious than pure gold."

Out of the corner of her eye, Lacy saw Sharon, her friend and administrative assistant, grimace.

"Sorry," Lacy muttered, realizing the statement was unusually raw even by her own standards. "Didn't mean to make you uncomfortable." She knew her brash, "tell it like it is" opinions often did just that to the people around her no matter how well they got to know her. However, Lacy couldn't help but softly add, "But it is the truth, darn it."

Always quick to recover from her reactions to her boss's outspokenness, Sharon grinned. "With all your big talk, a person would think you've had your bones jumped quite frequently.'' One of her delicate eyebrows arched. ''But you and I both know that the exact opposite is the truth.''

''Shh.'' Lacy lifted her index finger to her lips. ''Don't go spreading gossip that I'm a good girl. Not when I'm trying to get a man—*any man*—to father my baby.''

The two women shared soft laughter, but if the truth were to be known, Lacy didn't feel the least bit amused by her circumstance.

Frustration. That's what had her feeling so out of sorts this morning. Disappointment fairly pulsed through her veins. The magnitude of it almost—*almost*—overshadowed the ever-present echo that haunted her…the bone-deep ache that called out from her very soul.

Lacy wanted a baby. She *needed* to have a child of her own. And she knew that, at thirty-eight, her time was quickly running out. The tick, tick, tick of her biological clock seemed to grow louder with each passing day.

''I guess this gray cloud hanging over you this morning—'' as Sharon spoke, she went to the oak credenza and began organizing the contracts that Lacy had piled there to be filed ''—means your meeting with Mr. Fitzgerald didn't go well last night.''

A disgusted sound erupted from Lacy, and the mail she tossed on the desk went skittering and sliding across the wide glass top. ''The man acted as if I was asking for his right arm.'' She ran agitated fingers though her short locks. ''I offered him an iron-clad guarantee in the form of a legal contract stating that I would never ask him for monetary support. I have more than enough to give my child everything he or she might need.''

Sharon cocked her head to one side. ''You're a fantastic businesswoman. That's why Lacy Webs is so successful. Before you agree to create an Internet site for a customer, you make sure everything is signed and sealed.'' The woman's fist found her hip as she quietly pointed out, ''But you can't contract matters of the heart.''

''This isn't a matter of the heart,'' Lacy said. Unable to repress a sudden bout of humor, she chuckled as she quipped, ''It's a matter of the loins.''

''You're impossible.'' Sharon laughed, shaking her head as she returned to the filing.

Lacy sat pondering. She'd conducted her father-of-her-baby search just as she did her successful business: in a logical and rational manner. She'd developed a list of candidates, and approached each one with the common-sense plan she'd developed. But if Lacy had learned anything over the past months it was that, when it came to donating their sperm, men were neither logical *nor* rational.

Of course, more than one person had suggested she visit a sperm bank, but she simply couldn't see herself doing that. The mere idea seemed so cold. Not to mention the horror stories she'd read in the national news of women who had mistakenly been impregnated with the wrong sperm. No, thank you.

''Maybe you should think about getting remarried,'' Sharon suggested out of the blue. ''Husbands are much more receptive to fatherhood than single guys, you know.''

''I've tried happily-ever-after. I'm hopeless at relationships.'' The admission, and the defeated feeling it dragged along with it, had Lacy's voice rushing out in a husky whisper.

Poor Richard. The man—or their two-year marriage—hadn't stood a chance from the start. Not when Lacy silently-yet-constantly compared her husband to the most perfect man in the whole wide world...

Dane Buchanan.

Now, *there* was a man. Intelligent. Witty. Interesting. Athletic. Compassionate. Utterly fascinating. And more handsome than words could describe.

Lacy did her best to quell the euphoric shiver that washed over her when she remembered the chemistry she and Dane had shared all those years ago when she had been a freshman, he a senior, in college.

Certainly, if Dane knew about this cavernous ache tormenting her...if he was aware of this mothering instinct that relentlessly squeezed at her heart like a ruthless vise...he would understand. He would empathize. He would help.

Closing her eyes, she easily recalled the overwhelming electricity that coursed through her when Dane had touched her. *When he'd kissed her.* Even now as she sat at her desk, mere thoughts of the man made her skin prickle with awareness, made her heart thrum a staccato beat.

Thoughts of her perfect man had floated through her head often over the years. But lately, she'd found herself thinking of him during the day—and dreaming of him at night. Those night visions were becoming more and more sensual, more and more *erotic* each time she closed her—

The *clunk* of the file drawer closing startled her from her extremely corporeal musings.

"Don't worry," Sharon said, her hand on the doorknob as she prepared to leave Lacy's office. "There's a man out there just waiting to help you...a man who's perfect for your needs." The administrative assistant closed the door behind her as she left the room.

Lacy's lips parted in surprise, her eyes wide and staring. She was struck by the coincidence of Sharon's "perfect man" words aligning so completely with her own thoughts.

Coincidence? She blinked once, twice. That was no coincidence. It was a sign. A signal from fate. Hadn't she just had the thought that Dane would help her if only he'd known of her plight?

Why, for weeks now, her own subconscious mind had been sending her blatant hints in the form of frequent thoughts and lustful dreams of the man. Why hadn't she realized? Why hadn't she grasped the meaning of it all?

Immediately, Lacy turned to her computer, maneuvered the mouse and clicked the proper links that would log her onto the Internet. There had to be a way to find Dane Buchanan. There just had to be.

Hope sprang to life in her...a kind of joyous optimism, a gleeful anticipation that she hadn't felt in months.

Chapter One

An hour of torturous city traffic. Lacy groaned as she automatically reached to turn up the fan on her car's air conditioner. August was a killer month in Virginia. It wasn't actually the heat that made a person wilt like a cut flower, but the humidity.

She should have known not to rush out of town on a Friday afternoon. She should have waited until tomorrow morning when all the city employees were sleeping in and the roadways were clear. But she'd been too excited to wait a single minute longer to start her trip.

A mere two days had passed since she had pieced together her frequent thoughts of Dane Buchanan with her desire to have a child. In that time, she was able to find some sketchy information and a home address. But it had been enough to stir her excitement and get her on the road.

It was hard for her to imagine that her encounter with Dane had taken place nearly twenty years ago.

Encounter? A tiny voice in her mind questioned. It had been a date. A real, honest-to-goodness date complete with an end-of-the-evening kiss. A kiss, Lacy remembered, that had almost singed the wooden soles of the clogs she'd been wearing at the time.

Yes, but the facts of what had followed their one enchanted evening together were disillusioning. Dane had never called her. Never asked her out again, even though she'd blatantly suggested it. And when she had seen him on campus, usually in the library, she'd been the one who had made verbal contact. If she hadn't approached him, he'd have been content with a nodded exchange of greeting. Finally, she'd had to face reality. Dane Buchanan hadn't been interested in her in the least.

But that kiss...

How could he not have been as affected by it as she had been?

She sighed and gazed over at the map unfolded on the seat beside her. She still had a lengthy drive ahead of her.

To have discovered that he was still in the state had been a surprise. Lacy had explained to Sharon that Dane had the kind of intelligence that would have made him a hot commodity to businesses worldwide. If she remembered correctly, his major had been in one of the sciences. It would be easy to imagine him scouring the rain forests of the Amazon, hunting a cure for cancer. Or nestled away in a laboratory, inventing a new and phenomenal synthetic drug to be used as therapy for Alzheimer's patients.

Stories about him had raged through the students like a fire gone wild all those years ago. Lacy had been terribly curious. She'd been bold, too, even as a freshman. Her brassy confidence had her asking the senior out for coffee…an offer he'd surprisingly accepted. For hours they had talked while their coffee had grown granite cold.

Dane Buchanan, she'd learned after playing a tough game of twenty questions with the young man, had earned an academic scholarship to an Ivy League university. However, he'd chosen to attend a local college in Richmond in order to be near his ailing father. That information alone had been enough to melt Lacy's heart. He was president of the senior class, led the debate team to victory and was voted MVP of the football team. His dark good looks as well as his prowess on the football field led to his being approached by a New York modeling agency, and Lacy hadn't blinked an eye when he'd told her he'd turned down their offer for work. He simply hadn't seemed the type to flash his smile in front of a camera for money. Lacy smiled at the memory, his obvious embarrassment over the solicitation had been quite charming.

In that one short evening she'd spent with Dane in the café, she'd come to the conclusion that it would be easy for a girl to lose her heart to such a guy. He was everything a girl could want. He had brains. A ton of compassion. He was handsome as the devil. And when they had kissed good-night, Lacy had thought her toes were going to curl up into the arches of her feet!

Soon after that kiss, he'd mysteriously disappeared from the campus for nearly two weeks. And when he'd returned, it was as if their kiss had never happened.

Yes, he spent time with her in the library. On several occasions. He was always friendly, but at the same time, he never initiated contact, no matter how transparent she had made her own desire to date him.

Then a weekly newsmagazine had picked up Dane's all-around success story. The journalist had dubbed him the Perfect Man, and Lacy had had to agree. She'd considered asking him out on another date, but before she could, final exams were upon her and she never found the opportunity. He graduated. Left the school. And she never saw him again. End of story.

Surely he was married, Sharon had warned Lacy. And she'd had to agree. He probably was. And his wife was certain to have been a Miss America contestant who had given birth to a brood of beautiful children.

Still, something inside Lacy had her braving Friday-evening rush hour in order to drive into rural Virginia to see the man. Maybe—just maybe—Dane Buchanan would live up to his Perfect Man title and become the perfect father. For her child.

"Let's go into town for dinner tonight."

Dane Buchanan glanced at the slate-gray sky and then leveled his gaze onto his father-in-law's whiskered face. "Looks like rain, Alva. Weatherman's calling for a downpour. You know how that creek is. We should be here to check the herd. Besides, I've got two steaks thawed in the fridge for us."

"Aw, we have steak every Friday," the older man complained as he latched the door of the barn. "A little rain never hurt nobody. Let's chance it. Live a little. Couldn't you go for a plate full of Lottie's cheesy lasagna? I feel like some Italian food tonight."

Dane dipped his head, suppressing a smile. He loved the way Alva said that word...with a long *I*, like in *idea*. The whole population of Italy would probably have taken offense. But of course Alva meant none. He was simply a good-hearted southern boy who spoke just like everyone else below the Mason-Dixon Line.

He suspected Alva's hankering for pasta had less to do with lasagna and more to do with his wanting Dane and Lottie to have a chance to "keep company." His father-in-law would probably be surprised to discover that Dane had figured out his plan, but Alva had been trying to fix him up for the past year. Before Lottie, it had been Cindy at the post office. And before Cindy, it had been Lorraine, the organist at the local Methodist church. It was clearly Alva's opinion that Dane had been a widower long enough.

It was peculiar, Dane thought, that the father of the woman he'd married, the woman who had died so tragically because of his stupidity, would be doing everything possible to nudge other females into his path.

"Oregano upsets my stomach," Dane told Alva. "Upsets yours, too. And Lottie uses the herb rather liberally in her cooking. You know that."

"We could ask her to fry us some hamburgers. I'm sure she would." He nudged Dane with his elbow. "I think she's kinda sweet on you."

Dane just shook his head. "Steak and a baked potato will do me just fine. And I've got chocolate pudding for dessert." He pushed himself away from the fence and stretched the kinks out of his back, knowing full well his father-in-law would never be able to resist his favorite sweet. "But you go on into town, if you want."

"Nah, that's okay," Alva yielded. "Steak sounds good." His grin made his mouth go crooked, his eyes glisten. "I didn't know you made pudding. I'll just run on home and grab a shower. I'll be at your place in thirty minutes, so go ahead and fire up that grill."

Both men turned at the sound of tires crunching on gravel.

"Didn't know you were expecting company."

The candy-apple-red sports car had Dane's eyebrows drawing together with curiosity. "I'm not. You?"

The short exchange was silly, really. The men worked side by side every day. They had no secrets. If Alva was going to entertain a visitor, Dane would have known about it and vice versa.

The car came to a halt in front of Dane's brick rancher, about a hundred feet from where the men stood outside the door of the utility shed. A woman emerged from the automobile and made straight for the house, the sun haloing her short, flaxen hair.

"Woo-whee!"

Alva whispered under his breath, although at this distance there was no chance the woman could have heard him.

"Cute little thing, ain't she?"

Cute was an accurate description. But little? Dane nearly chuckled. Her body was as curvaceous as a country road, seeming to invite a man to meander along the soft hills and valleys. And she was tall. With yards of tanned, shapely legs that tapered into sexy ankles.

Suddenly the August air became so hot he thought

it just might scorch his lungs…*if* he could remember to pull a lungful of the stuff into his chest, that was.

"I'll take your stunned silence as a yes."

Alva laughed softly and gave Dane another poke with his elbow, breaking what could only have been described as some kind of strange, mesmerizing spell.

"She's most likely selling something," he grumbled. Dane did his best to hide the embarrassment he was feeling at being the butt of Alva's humor. "Probably wants me to buy a set of encyclopedias, or some magazine subscriptions, or life insurance."

"Well, boy," Alva advised, "you'd best go take care of the matter. I'm off to find a cool shower and some clean clothes."

His father-in-law's comment made Dane suddenly aware of the dirt on his jeans, the dust coating his hot skin. Why something so trivial should rear up to bother him now seemed unfathomable. He'd worked hard today. Just as he did every day. Sweat and grime came with the territory of running a cattle business. There wasn't much a man could do about that.

The woman was on his porch now, her hand raising to knock on the front door. Dane took a step toward the house.

"I'll see you in a…" His words petered out when he saw that Alva had already disappeared around the shed to take the path that led to his cedar-shingled bungalow just over the rise.

Long strides had him across the grassy patch standing between him and the front porch in no time flat. Shifting his hat back from his forehead a fraction, he called, "Can I help you?"

She spun on the narrow heel of her skimpy little sandal. "Hi," she said.

Her smile flashed bright as the summer sun, a direct contradiction to the steely clouds gathering overhead. Dane was struck with the oddest notion that he knew this woman.

"I'm looking for..."

The rest of her sentence trailed as she took a step toward him, recognition seeming to light her big blue eyes.

"Dane? Dane Buchanan?"

His heart jackhammered, and he wanted nothing more than to blame the long hours of hard work, or the heat from the summer day, but he'd be lying to himself if he did.

"You don't remember me, do you?"

Her voice had a lilting quality that started his memories churning—magnificent memories that he'd locked away in a vault years ago.

The pale pink lacquer on her long nails stood out against the royal blue of her blouse when her palm spread-eagled against her chest. "It's me. Lacy."

Lacy Rivers. His mouth seemed to draw into a smile of its own volition.

The years had changed her. She had filled out in all the right places. Cut off that glorious hair of hers. She looked polished. Businesslike. With a sexy edge that would drive a man wild. Much more sophisticated than the brash young woman in his memory.

The brash, fresh-as-a-spring-breeze girl who had nearly unraveled his well-laid plans all those years ago.

The thought thundered through his brain, crushing the warm, fuzzy memories, shocking the smile right off his lips.

"Lacy Rivers," she continued. "Please don't say you've completely forgotten me."

He took the steps slowly, doing what he could to gather his wits as he went.

All he was able to say was, "How could I forget?" He took off his hat with one hand and reached the other out to her. She took it in both of hers, and he couldn't decide if the sweat that prickled his forehead was from the oppressive heat and humidity...or the searing intensity of her skin against his.

Dane hoped like hell it was due to the soaring temperatures.

Her nails lightly grazed the outside of his wrist and the inside of his callused palm at the same time, and something deep inside him had him wondering how the hard length of them would feel on other parts of his body; his bare back, shoulders, arms and neck.

The notion so surprised him that he choked, jerking his hand out of her grip. He coughed once, and in an attempt to cover the awkwardness of the moment, he cuffed his fist against his chest.

"You okay?" Worry clouded her gorgeous sky-blue eyes.

"Fine, fine," he said, taking a step back in retreat. He felt an overwhelming need to put a little distance between them. So he could think. Try to make sense of these strange thoughts invading his mind.

"It's hot out here, and I'm feeling dry. I need something to drink." A stiff shot of whiskey was what he needed to steady this odd shock that had walloped him but good. He opened the screen door and inserted the key into the dead bolt. "Can I get you something? I've got lemonade. Iced tea. Beer—"

"A beer would be great." She pulled back on the screen door, taking the weight of it off his shoulder.

He twisted to face her, and she was so…close. The blue of her eyes was dazzling. The tip of her nose was appealing. The bow of her top lip was calling his name…luring him….

He swallowed. "Actually, it may be hot out here, but it'll be worse inside. I don't leave the air-conditioning turned on when I'm gone through the day. It'll take a few minutes for the house to cool off."

"Oh." She nodded. "In that case—" she took a backward step "—I'll wait here in the shade of the porch."

"Make yourself comfortable. I'll be right back."

He shoved open the door and, heaving a huge sigh, made his way through the living room and into the kitchen. He plunked his hat down onto the counter and turned on the water spigot. After he worked the soap into plenty of suds, he rinsed his hands and forearms. He splashed cool water onto his face and neck, and then took a moment to simply stand in the quiet.

All that could be heard was an intermittent splat as droplets of water fell from his chin and nose. He inhaled deeply. Exhaled slowly. But the chaos of his thoughts couldn't be held at bay for long, and curiosity had him shoving himself away from the sink. What was Lacy Rivers doing here? After all this time.

Well, he wasn't going to discover anything while he was hiding here in the kitchen.

He dried his face and hands, and then pulled open the refrigerator door. The beer bottles felt cool against his palms. On his way back through the house, he stopped to turn up the central air. Then he pushed his way back out onto the porch.

Perfect porcelain knees. That's what met his gaze the second he exited the house. She reclined in one of the two rocking chairs on the porch, her bare, sun-kissed legs crossed, one slender foot swinging lazily, the hem of her skirt rising just enough to offer him a tempting peek at her well-contoured thighs. The pale pink paint that coated the tips of her toes matched that on her fingernails and made her feet look delicate and sexy as hell.

Seemed as if all his eyes wanted to do was examine the cute little dimples below her kneecaps, rove over those lusciously sculpted calves, shapely ankles, narrow feet. He dragged his gaze to her face only to become enthralled by her full bottom lip, that perfect nose, her brilliant, azure eyes.

The woman was like a beautiful sorceress who had ensnared him in some sort of spell. But Dane knew the only enchantment going on here had to do with the curse of his runaway libido. It was as simple as that.

"You are finished for the day, aren't you?" she asked. "I'd hate to think I was keeping you from your work."

"The cattle are taken care of," he said, twisting off the top of one bottle and offering it to her. At that moment, he was struck by a thought. "I'm sorry. I should have brought you a glass."

She shook her head, her silky blond locks bobbing. "This is fine. Thanks."

He continued, "There's always some chore waiting to be done around the place. But I've put in enough hours. I'm all through for today."

"Good," she said, then glanced around her. "Nice spread you've got."

"Thanks." He lowered himself into the matching rocker, pausing long enough to take a swig of beer. The cold, yeasty brew felt marvelous rolling down his throat. "I'm half owner. My father-in-law owns the other half. We're partners."

"You're married?"

"Was. Helen died some years ago."

She murmured a compassionate response, empathy flooding her face, softening her already stunning features, and Dane thought his heart was going to jump right out of his chest.

He accepted her sympathy with a nod, unable to bring himself to reply further. That part of his life was hard to even remember, let alone talk about. The conversation sagged for a few awkward seconds.

"Those cows out there in the pasture sure are pretty," she said.

Dane couldn't stop the chuckle that erupted from deep in his chest. "I've never heard Black Angus described as pretty before. Strong, maybe. Healthy. But never pretty."

She lifted the beer, pressed her soft, glistening lips to the bottle's rim and took a drink. He couldn't take his eyes off the spot where her mouth met the smooth brown glass. Before he realized it, she was smiling at him again.

His tongue and throat felt as arid as a dusty cow trail, and he wondered if he was suffering a bout of sunstroke or something. What the hell was the matter with him?

Quick wit sparkled in her pretty baby blues. "I was only trying to offer you a compliment."

He nodded. "I appreciate it. We breed them, you know. So your praise is well taken."

Alva's beat-up truck rolled over the hill then, and Dane couldn't keep the surprise from his voice as he commented, "There's my father-in-law now. I'd better go see what he's up to."

He stood, and so did Lacy.

"If you don't mind," she said, "I'd like to use your powder room. I've been on the road a good while."

"Sure," he told her. "It's—"

"I'll find it." With a wink and a quick flash of a smile, she disappeared into the house.

That flirtatiousness caused a series of warm vibrations to trill through Dane's innards. He sucked air into his lungs, hoping to settle himself, and then he flagged Alva to a stop as he descended the porch steps on wobbly knees. Boy, oh, boy, his father-in-law would tease him for a month of Sundays if he got wind of the ridiculous reaction Dane was having to Miss Lacy Rivers.

"Where are you off to?" he asked Alva. "I thought—"

"I changed my mind," the older man said. "I want some lasagna. And I've reached the age where I should certainly have what I want. Hellfire, Dane, I might die in my sleep tonight, so don't try to talk me out of it."

Alva's ruffled feathers didn't fool Dane. He knew what the man was up to.

One of his eyebrows arched high as he accused, "So, you're just going to leave me here in the clutches of an encyclopedia salesman?"

The delighted sound Alva emitted could almost

have been described as a wicked cackle. "Sales-*woman,* don't you mean, boy?" He paused long enough to grin. "You should buy yourself a set of books. A little reading never hurt any man."

Dane only shook his head at his father-in-law's antics.

Then Alva's knowing gaze sobered. "But she ain't selling anything, is she?"

"How'd you guess?"

"Oh, I don't know," he said, eyeing the door of Dane's house. "The two of you looked…familiar sitting on the porch together as I drove up."

"Familiar?" Dane's forehead knitted. "That's a strange word to use."

Alva shrugged. "You do know her, though, don't you?"

"Sort of," he had to admit. "We went to the same college together. But that was a lifetime ago."

"So the two of you have plenty of catching up to do," Alva surmised. "You don't need me hanging around. And it's getting late. Be a gentleman. Invite the little lady to dinner. She can have my steak."

"You don't need to do this—"

"I told you," the old man interrupted Dane's protest, his grumpy tone back full force, "I feel like having Lottie's lasagna tonight."

Dane only shook his head. There was no changing the man's mind once it was set. "Well, I hope you've got some antacid tablets in your medicine chest. You're going to need them later."

"Aw, now, you know my stomach is clad in iron."

"You're gonna wish it was," Dane quipped as he stepped back from the truck.

More laughter rumbled from Alva. "You have fun chattering about old times."

The truck tires kicked up grit and pebbles as he pulled off down the lane.

Hunger pangs pinched Dane's stomach and he turned back toward his home. In that instant, Lacy opened the front door and stepped out onto the porch.

"It's got to be close to your dinnertime," she called to him. "Let's go into town and find something to eat." Then she added, "It'll be on me."

Her tone made him pause. That coaxing quality in her voice was enough to lead him to believe she was up to something. But that thought was pretty silly. He didn't even know Lacy Rivers. And she sure didn't know him. They hadn't seen each other in years and years. If she was up to anything, he sure was stumped over figuring out what it could possibly be.

"Maybe she does want you to buy some encyclopedias." He murmured the words under his breath as he started toward her, doing his best to contain the humorous grin that the idea churned up.

"Pardon?"

He did chuckle then, taking the stairs two at a time. "I said, you don't have to buy dinner. Besides, there isn't a decent meal to be had in Oak Flat."

"It is a small town, isn't it?" she commented. "As I drove through, I noticed a diner, a post office, a small grocery store and a church. Not much else."

"Sounds like you won't be needing the grand tour. You already took it."

"Hmm…I was hoping to find a hotel…"

He was vaguely aware of the concern shadowing her expression, but something more urgent called his attention.

What was that scent? An enticing, exotic aroma he couldn't put a name to. But whatever it was, it had his blood pounding. He swiveled his head, inhaling slowly, deeply, and he realized the perfume was floating on the air around Lacy. The sensuous fragrance made his gut tighten.

The sensation overtaking him was so...odd. He drove agitated fingers through his hair.

"I am hungry," he admitted, louder than he'd meant, wanting to focus on something—*anything*—other than her...other than the stirring and utterly unique scent of her. "I've got steaks for the grill, if you'd like to stay for dinner." He eyed her warily. "You're not vegetarian, are you?"

She grinned, and the dimple that formed in her left cheek caused a whirlwind of memories to buffet his mind. He remembered that sexy dimple. How he'd liked to make her smile just so he could see it. He remembered other things, too. The conversations they'd shared, filled with interest and fun. The utterly spontaneous laughter. The serious debates. *That kiss...*

He shoved the dangerous thoughts from him.

"I'm a meat-and-potatoes kind of girl."

"Good," he said. "We've got plenty of that around here. Let me fire up the coals, and while they're burning to embers, I'll grab a quick shower. Then, over dinner, you can tell me what brings you to Oak Flat."

Before too long he left Lacy Rivers in the kitchen washing the fresh greens that would make the salad she'd insisted on helping with.

In the bathroom, he stripped out of his clothes and turned on the shower. Full blast.

Memories bombarded his brain. The indecision he'd suffered. The worry. The temptation. The sleepless nights he'd spent praying for resolve. The fear that he wouldn't have the strength to do the right thing. But in the end he had. He'd succeeded in putting his own frivolous and selfish desires aside.

But Lacy had come back into his life. And as the cool water sluiced down his body, he couldn't help but conclude that he was once again experiencing the same reaction—or should he say the same *uncontrollable attraction*—he'd had to this woman all those years ago.

Chapter Two

The steak had been grilled to perfection. The baked potato was light and fluffy, drizzled with the perfect amount of rich butter. The salad was crisp and cool, the homemade balsamic vinaigrette making it utterly...perfect.

And so was Dane Buchanan. Just as perfect as she had recalled him being.

During her drive to Oak Flat, Lacy had worried that her memory of the man might somehow have been glorified by the passing years, that she'd made him larger than life in her mind. But she'd discovered over dinner that he was as honest, intelligent, hardworking and down-to-earth as she remembered. And there simply wasn't a more perfect physical specimen of a man to be found, she was sure.

His face was leaner, more honed than she remembered. The smile lines bracketing his mouth, fanning out from his eyes, gave him a remarkable appeal even her wildest imaginings had failed to conjure. His thick thatch of coal-black hair was shiny and Lacy found herself wanting to comb her fingers through the hints of silver at his temples. The years had transformed him physically into quite a man. Quite a man, indeed.

But what hadn't changed one iota were his eyes. She'd been fascinated by his smoky-gray gaze twenty years ago. Enthralled by the curiosity that had danced there, the vigorous light that flashed and caught her up in the energy that had seemed to pulse from him back then.

Those sooty orbs still ignited with uncontainable liveliness as she coerced him to tell her about his day-to-day life breeding and raising Angus cattle. He had a wonderful way of expressing the joy he found in what seemed the most mundane of chores. And she found herself just as swept away by him, just as mesmerized by his joie de vivre now as she had been when they'd attended college together. She listened in wonder as he described the spring calving season and all the sleepless anxiety and miracle of new life that came with it. And summer hay cultivation had kept him busy from sunup to sundown until just recently. He made the mowing, raking and baling sound almost fun, although she imagined it had to be hot, rigorous work.

A couple of times he'd tried to inquire about the reason behind her arrival, but she'd successfully parried his questions. She wasn't quite ready to blurt out her motivation for coming to see him. Not just yet.

Not only did she feel unprepared, but she also continued to be overwhelmed with desperation. The feeling kept rolling over her in a wavelike fashion. The anxiety welling in her brought a dread she wasn't used to. She was a successful businesswoman. And she hadn't gotten that way feeling apprehensive or fearful. She'd landed at the top by identifying terrific opportunities when they presented themselves...and by taking full advantage of those opportunities.

Dane Buchanan was the opportunity of a lifetime, in her estimation. But she couldn't allow this chance to slip from her grasp by shocking him with her request too soon. She needed to ease into this. Garnering his trust, renewing their friendship, had to come first. She had every intention of doing this right.

The other men she'd approached about fathering a child for her had been people she had known as friends, or through friends or her business. And those associations had helped her to make her plea, given her an opening, a place to start. But the connection she had with Dane was twenty years old. And she didn't even know how well he remembered their times together. How would the poor man react to having some stranger from his past marching into his home out of the blue, asking him for a sample of his sperm?

If she couldn't fathom the scenario herself, how in the world would he?

She needed to take her time. Ease into this.

However, the words that would incite his sympathy in her plight as well as obtain his help had better come to her. Fast. *Because,* her mind warned, *you don't have a whole lot in the way of time. You can only stall the man for so long.*

And as proof that the thought was nothing but dead on, he chose that moment to lean toward her, level a direct gaze on her face and ask, "So what was it that made you look me up after all these years, Lacy?"

Renewed panic swelled inside her. Frantically, she did what she could to tamp it down. But she could do nothing to quell the deep maternal yearning that plagued her soul. Her success here was more important to her than any business venture she'd ever strived for, any success she'd ever achieved.

Lacy literally blanched at the thought. She knew how intense, how terribly profound, her longing was to become a mother...to birth, to hold, to care for, to raise, to love a child of her own. She'd described it to her friends as being marrow-deep. But the fear pulsing through her at this moment, the chill the thought of failure brought, made her recognize that filling this hole in her, satisfying her mothering instinct, was more important than anything she'd ever needed or done or accomplished in her whole life. In that instant, she realized she'd never be complete without a child.

She also realized the extreme anguish she faced...if Dane were to refuse her request.

His gray gaze had darkened with concern as he reached across the table, his work-roughened palm warm, almost comforting, as it slid over top her hand.

"Are you okay?" he asked. "You've gone quite pale."

The physical contact made her blink, and she forced her eyes to remain open as she battled the wave upon wave of energy that coursed up her arm— over every inch of her skin—as her body reacted to his touch.

Her lips were cottony dry, and she moistened them.

She had no idea how long she'd been silent...or how long she'd been wrapped up in her own desperation.

"I'm all right." She picked up her glass of water, noticing the slight tremble of her fingers, and took a gulp. "You must think I'm crazy," she said after setting down the glass. "Coming here unannounced. After so much time."

"I don't think that at all." He relaxed against the back of the kitchen chair. "I will admit to being curious. I mean, it has been a lot of years."

She paused a moment, her mind going completely blank. How could she ever explain herself to him? He was going to hear what she had in mind, and he'd go screaming and running into the night. When they had sat down at the table to eat, rain had begun to ping against the kitchen windowpane, but Lacy doubted the weather would stop the man from fleeing the situation should he decide to do so.

Dane was sure to react adversely to her idea. All the other men had, hadn't they?

She wanted to give herself a swift kick. She wouldn't get anywhere thinking such negative thoughts.

With her eyes glued to the window, she murmured, "You see, I've been searching for the perfect man—"

His loud groan cut her words to the quick.

"You're not a journalist, are you?" he asked, suspicion varnishing his tone until it was sharp and burnished. "Twice over the years, I've had reporters hunt me down about that stupid article that was written about me during college. And I don't mind telling you, both times I've refused to be interviewed."

The subject of their conversation had twisted out of shape so suddenly that Lacy was taken off guard.

"No," she assured him. "I'm not here to do a story on you."

He looked visibly relieved. "That whole thing was such a crock. I can't believe that idiot reporter printed that story back then." Almost to himself, he said, "That silly article nearly kept Helen from marrying me."

"Well, I thought it was a wonderful article," Lacy told him. She couldn't have stopped the words from tumbling off her tongue even if she'd wanted to. "Very flattering."

"Too flattering," he spat out. "The adulation was so overdone that the whole piece bordered on obsequious. It was downright obnoxious with its sugary depiction of me and my life. If I'd have been diabetic, I'd have gone into insulin shock."

The venom that oozed from his words, his expression, his whole body stance, took her completely by surprise. Although she couldn't say why, his strong reaction annoyed her.

"But it was all true, wasn't it?" She blurted out the question, sure that she knew the answer already. "Every fact in that article was correct."

He refused to relent. "Come on, Lacy. *The Perfect Man?* No one is perfect. Especially me." His face screwed up as if he'd bit into something bitter. "The whole mess made me look damn pompous. I was relieved that the magazine hit the stands so late in the school year. I was never so glad to be away from a place as I was that university. That town. I'm not a conceited person, Lacy. And I hated being made to look like one.''

She fingered the linen napkin draped across her lap. ''It never dawned on me that you might feel that way about it. In fact, all these years I never imagined that you'd be anything but proud of the title.''

Dane shook his head. ''You have no idea how that title nearly ruined all my plans.''

As soon as Lacy heard the statement, she remembered how, when she'd made her final blatant attempt to encourage him to ask her out, he'd stressed to her his intent to carry out a certain plan he had for his life. She'd wondered about it at the time, but he'd kept his statements vague and she never did discover exactly what that plan involved.

''I arrived home after graduation,'' he continued, ''to find my fiancée waving that magazine at me and insisting that our getting married was a mistake. It took me six months to convince Helen otherwise.'' Under his breath he added, ''I've never been a violent man, but if that reporter had been within reach, I'd have beaten the daylights out of him more than once.''

''You were engaged back then?'' Surprise was evident in her tone, and she was terribly relieved that it masked the hurt that welled up in her.

His gray eyes averted from her face as he nodded silently, awkwardness seeming to settle on his broad shoulders.

The news was like a bolt from the blue—a bolt that burned and ripped at the very heart of her. ''When you took me out? When we…''

Kissed was the word teetering on her tongue, but

it petered out before actually forming. She felt stunned. Wounded.

"No." His answer was emphatic, his gaze conveying a steeling assurance as he shook his head. "Not when I took you out. But directly after."

For a moment, he looked as if he had more to say on the subject. But the moment passed, and he remained silent.

She remembered his disappearance after their date, surmised that this had been the time when their paths had veered from one another. What she'd wanted to do was ask, once he'd returned to campus, why he hadn't told her that he'd been spoken for. That he was in love with another woman. No wonder he hadn't nibbled any of the bait she'd tossed out at him. He'd been a fish that had already been caught. She felt embarrassed by the way she'd practically thrown herself at him all those years ago.

His words sunk into the chaos of her thoughts. *It took me six months to convince Helen....*

Why a man like Dane Buchanan would have to convince a woman to marry him was beyond Lacy.

"So we've ruled out the profession of writer," he said, reaching up to lazily scratch a spot on his chin. "What do you do for a living? You were such a go-getter, I knew you'd reach the top of whatever ladder you chose to climb."

She thanked her lucky stars that he seemed to have forgotten his original question regarding the purpose behind her showing up on his doorstep. Being no fool, she jumped on his question with both feet.

"I own an Internet consulting business," she told him. "Lacy Webs. We snare customers for you." She grinned as she recited the familiar words. "Our jingle. And, of course, our logo depicts a tiny spider in a frilly web."

He nodded, his eyes lighting with sincere interest.

"I worked for a computer firm for a few years. Then, I started building Internet sites for friends on the World Wide Web." She reached up and toyed with her small diamond stud earring. Finally, she shrugged. "My business just took off. Before I knew it, I had landed my first corporate account. My part-time, 'for fun' job turned into an instant career. I create commercial sites. For businesses offering services or selling merchandise online. Bank sites have sort of become my specialty. Although I've had my fingers in everything—hospitals, universities, retail chains. You name it." Her smile brimmed with satisfaction. "I've got more clients than I can handle, and I've been forced to increase my staff every year for the past five years. It's been great."

"Well, that's wonderful," he said, his words soft and genuine. "Like I said, I knew you'd go far. In whatever field you chose. I just knew it."

His praise made her flush with delight.

The reaction was funny, really. As well as surprising. She'd never felt the need for someone else's approval or admiration. Knowing her business was a success, and that she'd walked every step of the way on her own, that had always been enough for her. It might be silly, but hearing his good opinion of her made her feel, well, it made her feel…worthy.

The commendation he gave her not only felt nice, it revealed something to her as well. He'd thought about her. Maybe not often, but she'd been on his mind enough for him to decide these things about her. That idea thrilled the dickens out of her!

She didn't have time to stop and wonder why.

His slate eyes twinkled merrily as he leaned toward her again. "So, you never said what it was that made you think of me after nearly twenty years."

"I didn't, did I?" There it was again. That whirlwind of nerves churning in her belly. "W-well," she began, "as I said, I—I was looking for the perfect man…"

His handsome face pinched with something akin to physical pain. "And I already told you, he doesn't exist."

Emitting a weak laugh, she had to admit, "When I began my search for him, you hadn't yet come to mind, actually."

He looked surprised. As well as put in his place. She hadn't meant the remark in that vein, but he'd taken it that way just the same, she could tell.

"You see…" She reached up and smoothed her thumb over the shiny handle of the spoon sitting by her plate. "I'm working on…well, on this project. And I've been hunting for the perfect man…to…um, help me…reach my goal."

Dane remained silent and still, just waiting, and listening as she haltingly stuttered through her explanation. The intensity of his focus made her all the more nervous.

"I'd gone through every single male on my list," she continued. "And I was feeling pretty frustrated, too." Her chuckle was dusty dry. "It was kind of funny, really, how I finally came to the conclusion that you might be able to help me. I'd been thinking about you—''

And having these incredible dreams about you. But she didn't dare reveal that bit of information.

''—more and more often lately. And when Sharon…she's my assistant…suggested that surely there was a perfect man out there to fa—'' she caught herself in the nick of time, changing the word slightly ''—f-for my project. Those words…the perfect man…finally helped me to connect my subconscious thoughts of you with…well, with a possible answer to…th-this project I'm working on.''

From his expression, it was clear he wasn't feeling much more enlightened than he'd been a moment before. Why would he be when her clarification had been so darned convoluted and muddled?

''Lacy, I hate to tell you this, but I don't know squat about the Internet.'' He shook his head. ''I do have a computer. To keep the accounting records straight. But I've never logged on to the Internet, let alone surfed it, so I don't know how I could be of any help to you—''

''This doesn't have anything to do with the Internet, or computers for that matter.'' She stopped long enough to moisten her lips. ''It has nothing to do with my business at all.'' Adrenaline surged through her. Unwittingly, her chin dipped, and without even realizing it, she gazed up at him quite timidly. ''Dane, th-this is…this is—'' her throat convulsed in a swallow ''—well, it's personal.''

He watched her even more closely now. Then, without a word, he placed his elbows on the table, rested his chin on his laced fingers. It was a sign, she was sure. His way of indicating that he was paying strict attention to what she was about to say.

Thunder rumbled across the sky overhead. The rain beat harder against the glass. Lacy took those as signs, too. Ominous ones.

"There's no other way to say this," she began, "other than just...spitting it out." Anxiety prickled over her skin like a thorn-encrusted sweater, thoroughly flushing her with an uncomfortable heat.

This case of uncontrollable nerves was overwhelming as well as frustrating. She knew in her heart she wasn't a shy woman. She was bold. She was daring. Confident. But so much was riding on his reaction to the request she was about to make. He could so easily dash all her hopes with one small no.

But she wouldn't receive an answer, negative or affirmative, if she didn't explain her need to him. Pressing her lips together, she took a careful breath. She swallowed. And then she forced herself to reveal, "I want a baby."

Clearly, he tried to control his reaction. But she saw his spine stiffen, his eyes widen the merest fraction. A dozen different thoughts were crashing around in his head. She could see that by the astonishment raging in his eyes. He looked as though he was about to speak. But in the end he didn't. His forehead puckered and his head gave a slow, almost imperceptible shake.

"It's an overwhelming idea, I know."

"Overwhelming." He repeated the word, gazing off into a far corner of the room. When his gray eyes found her again, they were clouded with a myriad of thoughts and emotions. "Lacy, let me get this straight. You're asking me—"

"To father my child," she finished for him.

His chest deflated as he exhaled. His dark head shook yet again. "I know I'm not stupid. I guessed your meaning immediately, but having it spelled out doesn't make it any more believable, Lacy. Or understandable." His face expressed a mixture of shock and bewilderment. His shoulders lifted as he said, "I have to ask. Why me?"

"Because you're—"

Perfect, she'd nearly said. But she stopped herself, knowing now how much he had detested the description when it had been used years ago.

"—right." She left it at that. She whispered, "You're also my last chance."

"Oh, now…" He shoved his way out of the chair and paced to the counter, where he turned and stared at her. "Don't do that. Don't use guilt. That's not right. Or fair. I haven't seen you in—"

"I know. I know." She lifted her hand, palm out, hoping to appease him. Putting him on the defensive would do nothing to help her cause. "I was wrong to say that. I'm sorry."

His arms crossed protectively over his chest, his shoulders seemed to tighten, his whole body seemed to shrink from her. From the whole idea she was asking him to consider.

"This is crazy. Total lunacy."

She didn't know if he was speaking the words to her or to himself, so softly were they uttered.

"Dane, I'm thirty-eight," she explained. "Time is running out for me. My biological clock is ticking away. I'm surprised you can't hear it from where you're standing. Lord knows, I can hear it. Every moment of every day. My chances of having a healthy baby are dwindling with each month that passes.''

She could practically see the thoughts spinning in his mind.

Suddenly he blurted, ''You're a beautiful woman. Obviously successful. Why aren't you married?'' His gaze narrowed suddenly. ''You do like men, don't you? I mean, you *prefer* them?''

Lacy nearly laughed at his insinuation. But she didn't dare. She was certain he found nothing even remotely funny about this situation. Come to think of it, neither did she.

''Yes, Dane,'' she answered him quietly. ''I like men. I *prefer* them.''

''So—'' his hands flew up in the air and his tone rose ''—why aren't you married? Why aren't you going about this in the regular, normal manner?''

She sighed. Hadn't she been asked this same question over and over?

''I was married,'' she quietly admitted. ''It didn't work out. Richard and I...''

She let the sentence trail. Dane wasn't interested in what had happened between her and her husband. He was only interested in an answer to his question.

''I'd have loved to go about this in the conventional way.'' She paused, the wistfulness in her tone startling her. However, she was too intent on explaining her circumstance to dwell on what it might mean.

She continued, ''But that just didn't happen for me.'' As an aside, she softly offered, ''To tell you the honest truth, I think my success has a lot to do with the way I've been forced to go about this.''

Before she could say more, he blurted, ''Lacy, you don't even know me. Nearly twenty years have gone by since we went to college together. *Twenty years!* How do you know I haven't turned out to be a bad person? Why, for all you know, I could be a violent drunk. A brute. A derelict. Or a—''

''But you're not,'' she cut him off. ''Are you? You're none of those things. You're an honest, hard-working man. When we were acquainted in college, I knew you were intelligent, you were talented, you were energetic. A high achiever. I felt, then, that you could have reached the moon, if that's what you decided you wanted to do.'' Stubbornly, she tipped up her chin. ''And just as leopards don't change their spots, a man's DNA doesn't change, either.''

Her bravado had returned. The realization made her nearly giddy with joy and relief. That odd bout of shyness may have hindered her for a while, may have made raising the issue a little more difficult, but now that the topic was out in the open her fighting instincts had better rise to the surface or she was going to come away from this empty-handed.

Empty-handed. Glancing down at her bare and vacant arms, she was deluged with desperation at the thought of never holding a sweet baby. But she pushed the anxiety aside. Now wasn't the time for hopelessness. Now was the time for ultimate persuasion.

''Those great traits I knew you had—'' she looked him directly in the eyes ''—the traits I know you still have…I want them. For my child.''

She refused to act apologetic about what she would like for her son or daughter. Who didn't want a child who was creative and smart and talented and ambitious? Surely he would understand her feelings.

"But, but…" Obviously agitated, he turned away from her, raking his fingers through his hair. Then he faced her again, total incomprehension plain in his eyes. "How can you ask this of a total stranger?"

She sat for a moment, wanting—no, *willing*—the quiet, the stillness, to become noticeable. She must make him understand her feelings. The importance of this had to be made undeniably clear.

The seconds ticked by, but she didn't take her gaze from his. Finally, she unashamedly admitted, "Because I'm that desperate."

Chapter Three

Negativity. Denial. Refusal.

He was going to turn her down. That much was plainly expressed in the shadows clouding his eyes. Written on the taut planes of his handsome face. Drawn in the rigid lines of his body.

"Don't say no just yet." The words burst from her throat, the despair squeezing her tone sickening her as panic surged seemingly out of nowhere. "Let's clean up the dishes. Make some coffee." As she spoke, she rose and started snatching flatware, plates, glasses. "Didn't you say you'd made dessert? I'd love something sweet. How about you?"

She didn't dare look at him. Didn't dare allow her momentum to slow. She had to stay one step ahead of him. If she didn't, he'd surely catch up to her. He'd surely put a stop to all her hopes and dreams.

Whirling around, she raced to the sink. And as she set the dishes and cutlery on the counter, one of the water tumblers tapped against the edge of the porcelain sink.

Glass shattered, and Lacy was aware of pain. And blood.

A gasp escaped from her lips.

"What did you do?"

Dane was at her side before she had time to draw breath. And in that instant, it felt to Lacy as if the experience became dreamlike, surreal. As if she'd stepped outside her body, moved to the sideline to watch the scene transpire before her.

"It doesn't look too bad," he whispered, seemingly to himself.

The warmth of his fingers encircling her wrists. The worry planted in his forehead. The concern darkening his gaze to a steely gray.

Although she registered all these things—her body reacting, her heart melting, her knees quaking—she couldn't seem to make her muscles work, couldn't seem to voice the thoughts running through her head.

His touch was so gentle as he inspected the fleshy, outer pad of her palm that her heart warmed and tears misted her eyes. With his thumb, he tenderly probed the cut for any remaining slivers of glass. As he moved his way around the small wound, his gaze kept darting to her face, evidently checking to see if her expression conveyed any pain.

She was devastated by the compassion emanating from him. The urge to rest her head on his shoulder, to lean on him, to confide in him was awesome. Earth-shattering. She imagined a moment of complete peace in his arms...and for an instant, she could easily conjure what heaven really meant.

He reached to turn on the spigot. And when the

water hit the cut, pain stabbed across her palm, the sting of it snapping her out of her fuzzy, time-warp state.

Suddenly, she felt as if a firm hand had planted itself in the middle of her back and had shoved her, none too gently, back into the moment with all its panicky sensations churning in her gut and frantic thoughts swirling in her head.

He'd been about to say no to her request.

She made a weak attempt to pull her hand free from his grasp. "Let me clean up, Dane. I'll be just fine."

"Hold on," he told her.

But she insisted, tugging harder. "No. Really. I'll be fine. Just fine. I couldn't possibly not help you clean up."

Lacy knew she was babbling. Knew she was caught in a whirlwind of dread. But for the life of her she couldn't stop it, couldn't calm her thoughts. She knew without a doubt that if she paused, even for a second, he'd remember her request, remember his intentions of declining it.

That thought only caused the chaos in her to strengthen. What had been a mere storm of fear and dismay now mushroomed into a full-fledged hurricane.

Again, she made an attempt to tug her hand free of him.

And, again, he held fast.

Fat raindrops now pelted the windowpane like a hail of pebbles. Thunder rumbled. The kitchen had grown dark and dreary despite the overhead lighting.

"I really wish you'd just let me—"

"Lacy."

His voice wasn't loud, really, but his tone was firm. Firm enough to still her. Body, mind and soul.

The soap stung her wound, but she forced herself not to flinch. She held her hand perfectly still while he lathered her skin and then rinsed it under the running water. He reached for a clean dish towel, patted her hand dry. Then he picked up a fresh towel and wrapped it around her hand. He led her to the table and guided her into a chair.

She felt cared for. Calm. For the first time in... longer than she could remember.

He patted her shoulder. "I think you'll live." Then he smiled.

And Lacy was sure he'd hear the thumping of her heart.

"You probably won't even need a bandage," he continued. "But we'll keep an eye on it. You sit while I make coffee and clean up."

First, he popped a paper filter into the basket of the drip coffeemaker. The aromatic smell of ground coffee filled the air. He filled the glass pot with water and poured it into the reservoir. He switched on the machine and then turned his attention to the sink.

Carefully, he cleared away the broken glass. Then he rinsed the plates, bowls and cutlery and loaded them into the dishwasher.

All the while, he talked. Light and airy banter that, she was sure, was meant to clear the stress from the air. Her stress.

He talked about the worsening storm and what all the rain would do to the low-lying areas of the property. He talked about his house, and how he and Alva built it with their own hands. He talked about his close relationship with his father-in-law.

And little by little, by focusing on all of these mundane topics, Dane achieved his goal. Lacy's spirit stilled, and she relaxed. She enjoyed the sound of his voice. She enjoyed learning more about him.

The air was ripe with the rich scent of hot coffee, and he poured two cups. Then he served her a dish of pudding and set another at his place at the table. He stirred a dollop of milk into his coffee while she picked up her spoon and scooped some of the rich, chocolaty confection he'd served for dessert.

She rolled the cool, thick pudding around in her mouth and then swallowed.

"It's delicious," she told him. "I haven't eaten pudding in so long. I guess I always thought of it as a sweet for kids. But it really is wonderful."

She loved the way his eyes danced at the compliment.

"I add a secret ingredient."

Lacy had to smile. "You've got me curious now." Her tone lowered conspiratorially as she teased, "If you reveal all, I promise not to tell a living soul."

The manner in which he unwittingly cast a furtive glance over his shoulder, as if he really didn't want anyone to steal the mystery behind his delicious concoction, was too endearing for words.

"Sour cream," he said. "I stir in a hefty helping. That's what gives the pudding that rich sweet-and-sour bite. Good, huh?"

She took another bite. "Mmm," was her only response.

Dane sipped his coffee. "You still collecting baseball cards?"

The question surprised Lacy, and it delighted her

at the same time. To think that he'd remembered after all this time.

"I'm not, actually. Oh, I still have my cards. But I haven't added to the collection in years."

Talk of her collection made memories of her dad come to mind.

Lacy admitted, "I only collected them because my father was so interested in the game. He loved the old players. Mickey Mantle. Babe Ruth. Collected their cards. Our collecting them together gave us something...well, something in common. I sometimes believed my dad really would have rather had a son."

"Oh, I find that hard to believe."

Her shoulder lifted a fraction. "It's not something he ever came out and said. It was just a feeling I had. I think that's why I'm driven to succeed. I feel this need to prove myself." She shook her head. "I don't know. It's strange how the people in our lives affect us."

She'd have loved to tell Dane how he'd affected her. But now just wasn't the time.

"My dad died a few years back," she continued. "Esophageal cancer. He smoked all his life."

"I'm sorry to hear that." Deep compassion darkened his eyes. "How's your mom doing?"

"She grieved for my dad for quite some time," Lacy said. "But she's doing really well now. She's very involved with her church. She's on a cruise for elderly singles. She's sailing along the Alaskan coastline as we speak."

"That's great. I'm glad she's doing well."

Conversation lagged, and Lacy toyed with the pudding remaining in the stemmed dessert dish. The silence in the kitchen seemed so...loud.

Finally, Dane said, "You know, Lacy, we're going to have to discuss it sometime."

She sighed. And steeled herself. She was calm now. She was able to handle the rejection. When she looked at him, she knew in her heart that every desperate emotion she was feeling was displayed in her eyes.

"It's not like I'm asking you to sleep with me, Dane."

He didn't seem shocked by her statement. And it was clear that he empathized with her.

"I do understand that," he said, nodding. "I breed cattle, remember. I know a little something about artificial impregnation. That's not what—"

"Please," she said. "Don't say no right away. Think about it."

His mouth drew into a straight line, and his gaze brimmed with pity.

Finally, he shook his head. "There's nothing to think about, Lacy. I'm simply not comfortable with the idea. It's not something I could live with. Fathering a child…" He shook his head as the rest of the thought faded. "I'm sorry, but…I just couldn't do it."

Her heart wept a torrent of unshed tears—tears that sounded just like the rain pounding the roof overhead.

The quiet swelled. And if Lacy thought it had sounded loud and uncomfortable just moments before, it seemed positively stentorian now. The jangling of the telephone ripped through the silence at the exact moment that a bolt of lightning flashed and thunder boomed.

Lacy nearly jumped out of her skin.

The lights flickered, but remained on. Dane got up to answer the phone when it rang a second time.

To think how full of hope she'd been when she left Richmond earlier this afternoon. Now, all her optimism, all her anticipation, had turned to despair. Tears burned the backs of her eyelids. But she wouldn't let Dane see her cry.

Oh, she'd sob out her sadness. She'd mourn this opportunity lost. But that would have to wait. Until she was home. Alone.

"That was Alva."

Dane's voice was like the snapping of fingers, shattering her bout of self-pity.

"He's staying in town," he continued. "The state has issued flash-flood warnings."

Something in his tone told her he was preoccupied with other thoughts.

"You'll have to stay here tonight," he told her after a moment.

Stay here? The silent question nearly stole away her breath. Stay here in midst of the awkwardness of Dane's refusal?

No way would she even consider spending the night here.

"I have to go check the herd." He turned and went toward the front of the house.

"Wait!" Her purse sat on the kitchen counter and she snagged its handle on her way to follow him. Her only thought escape, she scrambled for her keys and was relieved that for once she didn't need to dig for them.

When she caught up to him, he was donning a rain slicker he'd evidently pulled from the living-room closet.

"There's no need for me to be in your way any longer," she told him in a rush. "Just tell me where the nearest hotel is. I have a bag in the car. I'd planned to spend the night—"

"You don't understand," he told her. "You can't go out in this."

Her forehead creased, her anger sparked. She couldn't help pointing out, "But you're obviously going out."

"I'm not driving. I'm going to check the herd. Make sure the animals found high ground."

Somehow, his answer didn't ease her ire, only ruffled it further. "Dane, this is silly—"

"It's anything but silly," he interrupted. He plucked the keys from her fingers, and before she even had time to draw breath, he said, "Don't move. I'll fetch your bag."

The wind whipped and thrashed, shooting needles of inordinately chilly rain through the open door. He pulled it shut behind him.

Don't move.

It wasn't the words so much as the commanding tone of Dane's voice that made her eyebrows arch high. Being ordered around wasn't something Lacy was used to.

Smoldering, she moved to the large picture window, but visibility was next to nothing and Dane was quickly swallowed up by the downpour. She heard the trunk of her car thump closed, then the sound of Dane's boots tramping up the front-porch steps.

He was soaked when he came inside.

"Take the room at the end of the hall," he told her, setting her bag by the front door. "The one with the green quilt on the bed. I've got to go."

He closed the door on the conversation, closed the door on the arguments she'd been about to make. After he was gone, Lacy stood by the window for long moments, letting the embers of her anger glow white-hot as she listened to the rain pounding the earth, the thunder rumbling across the blackened sky.

All was quiet the following morning. The rain had stopped. Yet, as soon as Lacy opened her eyes, she knew the storm hadn't moved completely out of the area. The air had that heavy feeling she'd always associated with precipitation, and when she slid from underneath the coverlet, she saw that the sky was dreary and overcast.

Last night, she'd realized pretty quickly that more was tied up in her feelings of anger than merely Dane's controlling orders that she'd be spending the night in his guest room. She'd had to admit that his refusal to help her become pregnant—her feelings of desolation and humiliation and rejection—had helped to fan the flames of her ire.

The storm had been vicious. It wouldn't have been safe to drive in the wild wind and rain. She'd known that. So after she'd allowed rational thinking to return, she'd picked up her bag and headed off to find the guest room.

She'd passed the master bedroom on her way down the hallway. And she'd have known it was Dane's domain even if she'd been blindfolded. The smell of him was unmistakable as she'd passed by. She'd been helpless against the urge to pause, to inhale the luscious scent, with its hints of cedar and leather, deep into her lungs.

The aroma had stirred something in her. Something

startling. Something deep and primal. But before she'd had the chance to really explore the mysterious emotions budding to life in her like slow-growing vines, the memory of his rejection had hacked the tender reeds at the roots.

She'd discovered two bedrooms at the end of the hall. One had been furnished with delicate white wicker. And on the dresser, she'd found a framed picture of a beautiful little girl whose hair and eyes were as dark as Dane's.

He'd spoken of a wife…Helen had been her name, Lacy remembered. Was it possible Dane and his wife had had a child? The picture, and the question, had made her terribly curious.

If he'd had a child, and he'd lost that child…

Grief swamped her and hot tears prickled the backs of her eyelids. How anyone could survive that kind of sorrow, that kind of heartache, was beyond Lacy.

Setting down the framed snapshot, she had picked up her bag and headed into the room across the hall, mournful echoes following close on her heels. She'd perched on the edge of the green-quilted bed, wondering about all Dane might have experienced over the years since she'd last seen him. He'd lost his wife. Had he lost his child, too?

The sad thought of his having lost a child mingled with her desperation to have one of her own. With the sound of the rain to muffle her tears, Lacy allowed herself to cry in despair.

But today was a new day. She rose and stretched, the feelings of defeat nowhere to be found. Now this was more like the Lacy she enjoyed being. Self-confident and positive. She'd find answers to her questions. She'd reach her goals. Somehow. Someway.

She'd thought Dane might be the solution to her problem. Well, she'd learned yesterday that he wasn't. Now was the time for her to pack her things and move on. And that's just what she was going to do.

After pulling on the single pair of jeans and the purple scoop-neck T-shirt she'd packed, she went into the kitchen looking for coffee. The note she found on the table stopped her dead in her tracks.

Went out to feed the cattle. Stay put.

That's all it said. Dane hadn't been polite enough to sign it. His only intention, it seemed, was to continue his ordering and controlling. The idea steamed Lacy. Made her forget all about her need for a cupful of caffeine-laden coffee.

Grinding her teeth, she went back to the guest bedroom, made the bed, put the magazine she'd borrowed right back where she'd found it, then snatched up her overnight case and headed for the door.

Keys. Dane had taken her keys.

She stood in the hall, fury seething through her veins.

Stay put, he'd demanded. Well, she'd show him she wasn't the kind of woman to be ordered around.

The man was nothing but an aggravation.

Stomping out to the barn to look for him—give him a few choice words—was her first thought. Then on a whim, she went into his room. She grinned when she saw her ring of keys sitting in plain sight on the dresser.

She snagged them with a satisfied sigh. No man was going to tell her what to do. The nerve!

The countryside was soggy. And remembering Dane's mention of flash-flood warnings, Lacy looked out toward the horizon, but couldn't see signs of high water. Puddles made getting to her car a little tricky, but she successfully avoided the worst of the mud. With her bag stowed in her trunk, Lacy got behind the wheel and started the engine. If she hadn't been so irritated by Dane's intent to control her, she might have felt badly about leaving without saying goodbye. As it was, her only thought was to get back home to Richmond and put this disappointing visit behind her.

Debris covered the narrow, one-lane bridge at the very edge of the property. Lacy slowed the car to a halt, pondering her next move. The only thing to be done was to clear the leafy branches and dead wood out of her path.

She frowned as her white canvas sneakers sunk into the red sandy mud coating the bridge. The creek water swirled and churned, lapping the wooden planks and even swelling onto the roadway at the far side of the embankment.

Lacy was wrestling with a particularly unwieldy limb, when a familiar battered pickup pulled to a stop at the far side of the bridge. She waved a greeting when she recognized Dane's father-in-law. She'd be grateful for his help.

However, before he reached the bridge, another vehicle approached, this one coming from the direction of Dane's house. The truck slid to a quick halt near her car, and Lacy's whole body felt electrified when she saw Dane emerging from the cab. Part of the reaction was a renewed sense of anger, but part of it was something else altogether. Something she didn't want to focus on too closely.

"And just what the hell do you think you're doing?"

Lacy gasped, shocked by the antagonism in Dane's tone. How dare he talk to her in that manner? Who did he think he was, anyway?

She felt her chin jut out. "I'm clearing a path so I can get away from you. That's what I'm doing." She wasn't certain, but she thought she heard something that sounded a lot like a snicker coming from the far side of the creek.

Dane trained his gaze on the elderly man standing on the other side of the bridge.

"And you're helping her? Have you lost your mind?"

"Don't you yell at him," Lacy butted in. "He just got here."

"She's right," the old man called out. "I just arrived from town."

Lacy found those livid gray eyes leveled on her once again.

"Didn't you see my note?"

"Oh, I saw your note all right. And if the two of us were alone, I'd tell you just what you could do with it."

Now she was sure she heard stifled laughter coming from Dane's father-in-law, the man doing his best to cover it with a cough that sounded terribly artificial.

Then Dane pointed at her, and her eyes narrowed. If there was one thing that grated on Lacy's good nature, it was being pointed at.

"If you and that fancy little sports car end up in the creek," he shouted, enunciating every other word by jabbing his finger in the air toward her, "don't you dare come crying to me!"

He turned then, got into his truck and made a quick three-point turn, spraying mud and muck all over the rear side panel of her car.

Lacy was so angry, she felt she couldn't breathe. Even though her chest was rising and falling, her lungs were pumping furiously, she felt as if she was deprived of oxygen.

"That man…" She spoke through gritted teeth. "That man…"

Lacy was keenly aware that she wasn't alone. More than anything, she wanted to spew out a slew of cursewords meant to cool her fury and vent her frustration. But she couldn't do that. Not with Dane's father-in-law within earshot, at least. Besides, that wasn't really her style.

"That man," she finally said, "is nowhere *near* perfect!"

Chapter Four

"His bark really is worse than his bite."

Lacy turned toward Dane's father-in-law when he spoke. The frustration stiffening every muscle in her body caused the smile she offered him to be tight-lipped. She took a deep breath, forcing all the antagonism that raged in her to seep away. In just a moment, her smile was more relaxed and much more friendly.

"I'm sure you're right," she told him, not sure whether or not she actually believed the words she spoke.

The old man approached her, offering her his hand. "I'm Alva. Alva Price. Dane's father-in-law."

Lacy pumped his hand. "Nice to meet you. Dane mentioned you yesterday when we talked. I'm Lacy Rivers. I went to college with Dane. I'd have driven back to Richmond last night if it hadn't been for the rain."

"That storm was something, wasn't it?"

"Sure was." Glancing down at her muddy sneakers, Lacy commented, "You really think the bridge isn't safe to drive over?"

Just then, Lacy became cognizant of scraping sounds of wood against wood under the bridge. The grating had been there all along, she guessed, but she'd been so intent on clearing the path, on getting back home, that she hadn't really noticed it. However, she couldn't help but realize what the sound was now. And what it meant.

The wind had knocked down branches, swept all manner of debris into the rain-swelled water. Anything could be jammed underneath the bridge, straining the supports, weakening the understructure.

Uneasiness crept over her.

Alva silently nodded toward the creek bank, then led the way off the bridge with Lacy following.

"It's probably safe," the man said, stopping only when he reached her car. "But I wouldn't chance it until we can check everything out under there, like Dane said."

The fact that Alva had left his truck on the far side of the bridge wasn't lost on Lacy. She nodded solemnly.

"So, how long will it take the water to recede?" she asked.

The man's gaze lifted to the horizon. "Well, the rain has moved up into the hills. Depends how long the storm hangs around up there, since that's where the creek originates. Also depends on how much water gets dumped by those storm clouds. Could be hours. Could be a day. Maybe two. Too many variables to say for sure."

"But I can't hang around here for a day or two."

Lacy dreaded the thought of facing Dane again, let alone being near him for forty-eight hours. "I have work to do. A business to run."

"It's the weekend," Alva pointed out. "Think of it as a little getaway. Everyone needs time away from the grind."

Not ready to give up on her idea of heading home just yet, Lacy asked, "Isn't there a back way out of this place?"

Alva pointed to the bridge. "That's the only way in or out."

"Well, what kind of fool builds a bridge that's at the whim of floodwaters on the only road that leads to civilization?" Immediately, she realized that Alva was half owner of the place. Her face flooded with heat.

She murmured an apology. "I was talking about Dane—"

"No offense taken." Alva chuckled, nodding his understanding. "But don't be too hard on Dane. There's a reason he gets so fired up about the bridge. See…the road might not look like more than a dirt driveway, but it is a tertiary road. Owned by the state. And the road commission won't allow us to build a better bridge. They say we don't have the expertise to do it. Yet, they also claim they don't have the funds to rebuild, either. It's frustrating. Still, Dane petitions for a new bridge every six months."

"I see where his frustration is coming from." Lacy smoothed her hands together. "But that's no reason for him to shout at me. All he needed to do was communicate that it might not be safe for me to cross."

"Seeing you standing on the bridge," Alva continued, his voice growing softer, "probably brought back some bad memories for him. You see, he lost his family—his wife and daughter—at this very spot during a flash flood several years ago.''

Lacy stifled a gasp, the chill coursing down her spine making it seem like the middle of winter rather than the hottest part of August. ''Your daughter?'' Immediately, the picture she'd found in Dane's house last night, of the dark-eyed little girl, came to mind, and she added, ''And granddaughter?''

Alva's face grew taut with an age-old grief as he nodded silently.

A lump the size of a walnut rose in Lacy's throat. ''Oh, my.'' Her voice sounded rough and rusty. So Dane had lost his baby girl.

''Now, don't go feelin' bad. There was no way you could know. I'm just tellin' you because I think you need to…well, to understand Dane's behavior. Something happens to a man when memories and anxiety begin to poke at him. Anger is often the reaction you'll get, but fear is the driving force. Dane didn't want to see you get hurt. That's what all his shoutin' was about.''

She glanced down the road toward the direction of Dane's house. She couldn't see his home, or any of the outbuildings, from where she stood. But she knew he was back there somewhere. Compassion stirred in her. As well as a deeper understanding of his behavior.

''I guess we should go back,'' she told Alva. ''Care for a lift?''

The elderly man grinned. ''I'd be obliged.''

''And while we're driving back,'' she quipped, rounding the car and opening the driver-side door, ''maybe we can both send that storm front some positive energy that just might encourage it to move on in hours rather than days.''

Alva's knee-splitting laughter made Lacy chuckle, despite the thought of having to face Dane.

''I'll be happy to send energy, prayers, alms or whatever else you've got in mind,'' Alva retorted as he got into the car and shut the door. ''But I doubt that either one of us is powerful enough to affect Mother Nature.''

Lacy's mouth screwed up comically and she sighed heavily. ''You're probably right about that, too. But it won't hurt to try.''

The old man chuckled yet again. ''It sure won't hurt to try.''

''That Lacy sure is a feisty little lady,'' Alva said later that morning.

Dane glanced up from the bag of cattle feed he was wrestling with inside the barn. ''She's still here, then?''

Alva nodded.

''I'm relieved to hear that the stubborn woman has some common sense after all.'' He cut open the bag and dumped the feed into the trough.

''Aw, now—'' there was censure in his father-in-law's tone ''—no need to be like that. She only got riled up because you were acting like a half-raised heathen with all that yellin' and arm-waving. I'm sure she'd have been reasonable if you'd only offered her a simple—''

''Reasonable?'' Dane tossed aside the empty feed sack. ''Let me tell you just how reasonable Lacy is. She came here because she wants to have a baby. My baby. How reasonable does that sound to you?''

A certain amount of smugness straightened Dane's shoulders when he saw that his father-in-law was shocked into complete silence.

Finally, Alva whispered. "Did you say baby?"

"That's exactly what I said. However—" now his tone turned sarcastic "—that is all she wants from me. Just a teeny sample of my sperm, is all she's asking for." Just thinking about it made his neck and shoulder muscles knot. He grumbled, "She was talking about me and my genes as if I was prime bull stock rather than a flesh-and-blood human being."

Something about explaining this situation to a third party had Dane feeling somewhat humiliated. He felt his cheeks warming with embarrassment.

Luckily, Alva didn't seem to notice. His father-in-law's reaction came in the form of a long, incredulous whistle.

"Whoa. And here I thought the two of you were spending a pleasant evening catching up on old times."

"Things did become a little awkward last night," Dane admitted. "In fact, at one point I actually felt sorry for her." His tone lowered as he said, "Her need for a child seems almost…frantic."

Immediately, he felt guilt closing over him, and he regretted having voiced that last bit. He probably shouldn't be revealing what might be Lacy's deep, dark secrets.

However, he was once again flooded with compassion as he remembered when she cut herself on the broken drinking glass last night, and how she seemed to barely register that she was bleeding, evidently so upset had she been by the mere thought that he might refuse to help her.

She'd felt so tiny—so needy—when he'd taken her hand in his and checked to see if she had a piece of glass in her small wound. The urge to hug her to him, to tell her everything would be okay, had been overwhelming during those moments. He'd cleaned the cut, and he remembered how his gut had tightened as the pad of his thumb roved over the velvety indentation of her palm. Her hand had been soft and supple compared to his callused skin.

The extremely corporeal reaction he'd had to Lacy had taken him aback. As quickly as possible he'd told her to sit at the table while he busied himself washing dishes and talking her ear off. The steady conversation had been meant to achieve a twofold goal; he'd wanted to soothe the tension in her, and he'd also been desperate to still the need that had surged through him when he'd touched her shoulder, her milky wrist, her hand, her soft, slender fingers.

Her skin was like fresh cream; lusciously rich, silky smooth and pearly white. At one point, the sight of the delicate underside of her wrist had beckoned to him, and he'd nearly lifted it to his nose for a sumptuous sniff, to his mouth for a transient taste.

The memory of those few seconds they'd spent standing close together at the sink made his mouth go as dry as the cracked corn kernels he'd just dumped into the feeding trough.

He huffed out a breath, realizing suddenly that his father-in-law had grown mighty quiet. He shoved Lacy's image from his mind and looked at Alva. The man's unreadable expression was disconcerting.

Dane gruffly said, "One thing is for certain—" he grabbed another bag of feed, hauled it to the trough and slit it open "—no matter how desperate Lacy Rivers is, she won't be having *my* baby."

After witnessing his tirade at the bridge earlier that morning, Lacy wasn't sure how Dane would act when he finally made an appearance at the house. She was terribly relieved when he greeted her civilly as he entered the back door. She was standing at the kitchen counter slicing a tomato that she'd found sitting on the windowsill.

"I took the liberty of making us sandwiches for lunch," she told him.

"Sounds good. I'm starved."

"Will your father-in-law be joining us?"

Dane shook his head. "Nah. It's our habit to eat lunch apart. We spend too much time together as it is. Does a person good to have a little time on his own."

Lacy sensed Dane was attempting to relay a witticism regarding his relationship with his father-in-law, although there wasn't a trace of humor in his tone. It was obvious that he was feeling as awkward as she about her being here, about the words they'd exchanged at the bridge.

He bent over to untie his leather boot laces. "It'll only take me a minute or two to get cleaned up. It's pretty muddy out there after the rain."

His worn jeans hugged his rump as he wrestled to get the boot off his foot. Lacy's gaze latched onto his firm gluteus. His thigh muscles tensed and relaxed, playing beneath the soft, worn denim. Her blood heated. Thickened. Throbbed through her veins. She felt flushed. All over. Before she had time to train her eyes on something—*anything*—else, he straightened and looked directly into her face.

Like a wide-eyed and inexperienced thief who had been caught clutching a handful of stolen jewels, she scrambled for something to say, something that might save her from the embarrassment of the moment.

"I'm sure you're used to a hot lunch," she blurted, her face igniting like fire. Surely she was about to faint into a large heap right on the kitchen floor. "Since you work so hard and all. But, well, I guess you should know, I'm not much of a cook." She fumbled with the juicy tomato slices, focusing on placing them neatly on top of the ham and cheese and lettuce.

"Sandwiches are fine. I appreciate your going to the trouble to make them."

Luckily, there was nothing in his voice to hint that he might have noticed her inappropriate staring. Ogling, really, she silently but honestly admitted to herself. Her relieved sigh was actually audible. She was aware that he passed her on his way out the kitchen door, the wood-and-leather scent of his cologne mingled with the pleasant smells of warm hay and fresh rain. And she was startled by the overwhelming urge to follow the appealing outdoorsy aroma right on down the hallway. Thank goodness her feet had enough sense to remain rooted to the kitchen floor. The bathroom door closed, and before too long the water faucet turned on.

In the silence of the kitchen she realized it wasn't the outdoorsy scent that attracted her as much as it was the outdoorsy man. Before today, the men she'd dated had been suit-clad corporate types. Stuffy men who got themselves in a tizzy if they accidentally dripped tomato sauce on their ties or jackets. Dane spent his life in the fresh air and sunshine. The idea of tramping through high grass or puddles of rain and mud didn't faze him in the least. For some unfathomable reason, Lacy decided Dane came out way ahead in the contrast. In fact, his independent, man-against-nature lifestyle made her heart flutter.

Her mouth screwed up at one corner. Again, she was forced to concede that it wasn't the lifestyle. It was the man.

Moving the food-laden plates to the table, Lacy wondered how on earth she could feel so attracted to a man who could be so insufferable as Dane had been earlier. When he'd shouted at her this morning, she'd wanted to call him all manner of names. But Dane's father-in-law's presence at the bridge had forced her to tame her tongue.

And the information Alva had revealed about Dane's past had made her very happy that she hadn't given her usual bluntness free rein. The man had endured a loss that had resulted in some deep emotional scars, and that's why he'd acted as he had. Those scars were cause enough to have him anxious about someone else getting hurt or killed because of the weather and the flooded bridge. Lacy was actually relieved that she hadn't acted on the anger he'd stirred in her.

When she'd first returned to Dane's house with Alva this morning, she'd gone directly to the bedroom where she'd found the picture last night. The little girl had been beautiful. Angel was the image of Dane, with her dark eyes and hair. How it must have wounded him to lose her. And his wife. What grief he must have suffered.

However, on the other hand, she couldn't help but

think how truly blessed he was to have known the joys of being a parent. He knew what it felt like to have a child wrap her little arms around him. He'd experienced seeing his little girl take her first step, speak her first word. To see the love he felt for his child reflecting in her angelic, shining little face.

The bliss of it rushed at Lacy. Made her eyes sting with tears. Oh, how blessed he was to have experienced those things.

How on earth had he endured the agony of her death? she wondered. The mere thought of loving and then losing a precious daughter stole away Lacy's breath. And to think that she'd arrived on his doorstep with the intention of asking him to father another child, yet to never see that babe take a step, to never hear a single coo, to never feel a soft and silky hug. Was she really that cold and heartless?

What she needed to do was go home and leave this man alone. That was the moral thing to do. The right thing to do.

Dane returned to the kitchen, and the two of them sat down at the table to eat. His small talk was benign and friendly, reflecting his obvious willingness to forget the harsh words they'd tossed at each other earlier.

Somewhere into the second half of her sandwich, she leveled her gaze across the table and said, "Dane, I'd like to apologize for this morning. I honestly didn't realize that crossing the bridge might be dangerous." She took a small bite of ham and Swiss cheese, savoring the chewy rye bread, and swallowed. "And I am sorry I didn't follow the instructions you left in your note telling me to stay put." The smile she offered was filled to the brim with irony. "It's just that I'm not used to following orders, you see.

Back in Richmond, I'm the boss. I'm the one who gives the orders.'' The humor in her tone metamorphosed into gentle chiding as she added, ''It would have been better if you'd have taken the time to explain about the swollen creek and the bridge.''

She could barely believe the patience she'd used in explaining her actions. Usually, when her nose got shifted out of joint by a man's behavior she simply told him he was an idiot and that would have been that. No explanations. No apologies. But this time was different. Dane deserved to be treated more gently now that she knew about the grief he'd experienced. It was important to her that Dane understand that she honestly hadn't realized how unsafe her intention to cross the bridge had been.

His dark head bobbed, and he wiped his mouth with a napkin. ''You're right. I should have explained. It's just that the bridge…it's a touchy subject with me.''

Now it was her turn to nod. ''Your father-in-law told me what happened on the bridge. To Helen and Angel. And I'm terribly sorry. About the accident. And I'm also sorry if seeing me on that bridge gave you a fright. I sure didn't mean for that to happen.''

''I know you didn't.''

And, evidently, that was all he planned to say on the matter, even though she suspected there were plenty of thoughts swirling through his mind. She could guess his turmoil. She imagined the whole ordeal bothered him more than he was able to convey. She decided it was best for her to let the past remain where it was for now.

''Listen,'' she said, ''since I'm going to be here anyway, why don't you let me help you this afternoon? I couldn't possibly sit around for hours and do nothing. I'd go stir-crazy. I've never worked with cattle, but I can at least be an extra pair of hands. What do you say?''

He grinned, and Lacy felt her heart hitch in her chest. My, but he was a handsome man. She noticed the size of his hands as he brought the sandwich up to his mouth, and she remembered how strong and sure his fingers had felt against her skin as he'd gently ministered to her cut last night. Something similar to stardust skimmed and skittered over every inch of her flesh.

''It's nice of you to offer,'' he told her. ''But most of the work is done for today. I take it easy on the weekends. I was planning on just riding the fences this afternoon. Boring work, but it's got to be done every once in a while.''

''I'd love to go. Think Alva would mind me tagging along?''

''I usually do this job alone.''

''Oh.''

''But I wouldn't mind company today. Do you ride?''

''Horses?''

White teeth flashed when he chuckled at her blurted question. ''Well, I hadn't intended on carrying you piggyback.''

''I thought we'd take your truck.''

''We could,'' he said after he'd swallowed his last bite of lunch. ''But it would be an awfully bumpy ride. Besides that, it's wet out there. We'd spend most of the afternoon getting ourselves out of the mud. If you're scared of riding…''

''Who said anything about being afraid?''

He rubbed his fingers over the lower part of his face and Lacy knew he was trying to control his laughter. ''I didn't mean to offend you.''

She ignored the fact he was trying to make amends. All she saw was the challenge that had smacked in his words, in his teasing.

''I'll ride. I'd like to try.'' The instant the words were out of her mouth, anxiety reared its ugly head and she was forced to ask, ''Are the horses gentle?''

''Very,'' he assured her. ''But you can't ride in those.'' He pointed under the table at her sneakers. ''You need a little more protection. Go into the mudroom and find yourself a pair of boots that fit while I clean up the lunch dishes.''

''Yes, sir.'' She'd nearly saluted him, but thought better of it. It was her aim to make friends. After what she'd learned today, she imagined he could use one.

They rode the fence line for what seemed to Lacy to be hours. The horse she was riding was docile, but she was amazed at the amount of muscle it took to guide the animal where she wanted it to go. Her thighs and buttocks had begun to ache nearly an hour ago, and now they were screaming at her.

But she'd be darned if she'd complain to Dane.

Time and again, she'd found herself trailing behind him. And no amount of pain and suffering was enough to keep her from noticing how tall he sat in the saddle, how broad his back was, how his muscles bunched under the fabric of his white cotton shirt.

At one point, her brain had clicked into some sort of auxiliary mode, and she'd begun to fantasize about riding double with him, wrapping her arms around his trim waist, laying her head against his back as the horse's gait caused them to rock sensuously back and forth, back and forth, her inner thighs rubbing intimately against him.

The daydream had been a marvelous way to forget all about her own throbbing muscles. But then her mind went so far as to imagine Dane pulling his horse to a halt, hopping out of the saddle, reaching to tug her to him, and she tumbled into his rock-hard chest, his lips lowering to crush against hers in a kiss that was—

Startled by the utter eroticism, Lacy blinked the vision from her thoughts and prodded the chestnut bay into a trot. The beautiful bay Dane had introduced as Bo had whinnied, cutting his head to try to get a glimpse of the crazy woman on his back. Lacy tried to reassure him by stroking his soft, brown neck.

She was tired, and in pain, she silently reasoned in an attempt to explain away the sensual impressions her thoughts had conjured. She would enjoy a break from the saddle...but only to give her body a rest, not so that Dane could swoop her into his arms and kiss her passionately.

Who are you kidding? a quiet voice mocked her from somewhere in the back of her brain.

Lacy was never one to lie to herself. Okay, so she found the man attractive. Okay, so she wouldn't mind if he pulled her against his chest and kissed her breathless. She wouldn't even have any trouble returning such a kiss, either, if he were to gift her with one.

Why should she? He was a gorgeous hunk of a cattleman. And the way his hips and thighs and rear moved in that saddle had her blood thrumming like the strings of an acoustic guitar. The very sight of him controlling that animal with his strong legs was enough to spark erotic thoughts in any red-blooded woman.

Those jean-clad thighs tensed yet again as he softly crooned, "Whoa, boy," to Jasper, his gorgeous brown-and-white quarter horse, whose patchy coloring he'd earlier described to Lacy as skewbald. Dane pulled back on the reins. To Lacy, he said, "Let's take a break."

"Sounds good to me." It took her a second or two longer to get Bo to comply with her wishes. Dane had already dismounted and was standing next to Jasper by the time she finally succeeded in stopping.

Her muscles were so stiff that when she straightened her knees and made to dismount, pain shot through her thighs and the small of her back. She plopped back down into the saddle, barely able to contain the groan that gathered in her throat.

"Looks like you need some help."

Was that teasing twinkling in his tone? At this point she really didn't care. All she wanted was off this horse.

Lacy sensed that her smile looked more like a grimace. "I wouldn't say no to that."

Again she stood in the stirrups, and she felt his strong hand, warm and supportive, encircle her knee as she lifted her leg over the animal's body. Then both his hands snuggled her waist, holding her firmly until her toes touched the ground.

She turned then, looking up into his smoky-gray eyes. The heat of his body was overwhelming. The warm smell of cologne and leather and horse wafted and swirled around her. Tiny currents zipped and buzzed, jolted and shocked, as if last night's storm

had left behind some remnants of electricity in the air
to stun them.

He was fully aware of it, too. She could plainly see
by the look in his eyes, in the tension around his sexy
mouth.

Something stirred in his gaze. Need. Desire. And
her breath quickened, her chest rose and fell as she
inhaled and exhaled what seemed to be great quan-
tities of oxygen. Yet, she still felt light-headed and
dizzy. Deprived.

The temperature seemed to rise several degrees,
and the day brightened, although Lacy was clearly
cognizant that the clouds in the overcast sky hadn't
thinned one iota. It was as if the sun was aiming
shafts of pure white light down on them. But in reality, the weather made that impossible. She knew
that. Still…

Neither of them moved. They didn't blink. They
didn't breathe. In that instant, they had both become
frozen in time.

Chapter Five

His eyes were the deep, rich color of a dove's wing, his gaze feather-soft as he stared into her face. Lacy felt as if they were closed up in a vacuum with no air to breathe. The intensity of the moment was soul-shattering. And there was no way either of them could deny that something utterly amazing had chosen that moment to settle over them.

Without a word, he reached up and slowly ran his rough fingertips over her cheek, along her jaw. His callused skin felt decadent, raw, deliciously erotic against her flesh, and she tilted her face to meet his touch. Her hands rested lightly on his biceps, and she marveled at the solidness of him, the muscle and sinew. She was aware of a feverish heat, but didn't know if it was his body or her own that seemed to smolder like embers.

Something flickered in his gaze, some shadowy emotion she couldn't put a name to.

''I can't do this,'' he murmured.

Can't do what? she wondered. Momentary confusion short-circuited her thoughts. Then she remembered. The baby. Her baby. The one he'd refused to help her conceive.

"You already said that last night," she reminded him softly, her tone grating, as if it had been baked dry by the August temperatures…or by the searing heat radiating from whatever it was attempting to consume them both.

"I don't mean the baby. I mean—" he paused long enough to swallow "—this."

Of course, he hadn't been talking about the baby. He'd been referring to…this. This thing between them. This palpable, breathing, almost tangible thing that had them both sweltering and…and helpless. How could she not have realized that? How could she have thought he'd been speaking about anything else?

What encased them so firmly was more than mere emotion. More than simply the sensation of two human beings feeling attracted to one another.

Allure. Temptation. Fascination. None of those words seemed to fit the height and depth and breadth of what was pulsing between them at this instant. It was so huge, so frighteningly real, that it seemed to be an entity with a life of its very own.

"I don't have a clue what the hell this is."

Although his tone was soft, the harshness in it startled Lacy.

"All I know is that I've been aware of it since the moment you arrived on my doorstep."

He was right. Whatever this mysterious thing was that held them captive like bands of steel, it had been present since they'd first laid eyes on each other yesterday, after so many years apart. She'd been conscious of the feeling of being rocked to the marrow of her bones by seeing him again after being separated from him for so long. However, he'd seemed so nonchalant, so relaxed when she'd arrived, that she was surprised to hear him admitting he'd noticed anything at all.

But he had noticed. As had she. And this thing seemed huge. Alive. Bigger than both of them.

So…where did they go from here?

Bo snorted softly behind her. A bird twittered melodically in a tree not too far away.

"Look, Lacy," Dane said. "You weren't in my plan twenty years ago. And you're not in my plan now. You need to know that I can't…do this."

It seemed to frustrate him that he couldn't find the words to describe the situation he was in, the feelings he was experiencing.

When he turned and took that first step away from her, Lacy felt as if the seal of the vacuum she'd been trapped in was broken, and air, cool and clean, washed over her. She inhaled it deep into her lungs. She felt suddenly chilled.

Then, as she realized what he'd said, she blinked. And frowned. She took a step toward him and winced as pain shot through her overtaxed muscles. For a moment, she'd forgotten all about how sore her legs and torso had felt when she'd been riding Bo.

Without even realizing it, she must have sucked air in through clenched teeth because, over his shoulder, Dane said, "We'll walk some. That'll help ease your stiffness."

With Jasper's reins in hand, he set off over the field. Lacy grabbed her horse's lead and started off after Dane.

"Hold on," she called, her gait looking and feeling more like an old woman's hobble. "What did you mean by that? What you just said…about my not fitting into your plan twenty years ago."

From behind him, she watched as one of his broad shoulders hitched in a shrug.

"I meant just what I said. You didn't fit into my plan then, and you don't—"

Close enough to him to pinch at the fabric of his shirt, Lacy tugged hard enough to force him to stop. "But the way you said it…your tone, your inflection…leads me to believe that our relationship back then…" Her voice trailed, and then she corrected, "That our *friendship* might have threatened that plan you always talked about so much." Then, almost to herself, she added, "Well, you talked around it, actually. You never really explained it to my satisfaction."

"If you only knew," he said, shaking his head and walking several more paces.

Something in his voice, in the stiff set of his shoulders, had her hobble quickening to a shuffle. She wished she could see his face.

"Knew *what?*" Her tone rose an octave as she hurried forward as quickly as her screaming muscles would carry her.

"How much you threatened my plan."

He stopped then, pulled off his hat, swiped his forearm across his brow. This pause gave her time to actually catch up to him, look into his eyes.

"I did?" The amazement exuding from the tiny query should have been comical, but the overwhelming importance weighing on the two small words held her amusement at bay.

Dane nodded. "You did."

For a moment, she was speechless. All those years ago, she'd thought he hadn't been the least bit interested in her. Now she was discovering that she'd threatened his well-laid, all-important plan.

Finally, she quietly asked, "So how come you never said anything?"

His laugh was humorless. "That would have only made matters worse, don't you think?"

For him, maybe, she thought. But it would have done wonders for her own self-esteem.

"For years," she said, "I thought there was something wrong with me. Something that kept you from wanting me." In some unspoken agreement, the two of them started off over the field again. "For a while I went through my 'too tall' stage. I wore nothing but flats thinking maybe guys liked women who were smaller, more vulnerable. Then I went through my 'too short' stage, and I wore sky-high spiked heels. After that, I thought I was too skinny and too fat, too smart, too dumb, too loud, too quiet. Heck, Dane, by the time I was finished psyching myself out, there was nothing left for me to try. No fad I hadn't gone through. No phobia I hadn't suffered."

He face twisted up in a grimace. "All because of me?"

"What can I say? I had the hots for you. And when you didn't take notice of me, I immediately thought it was something I had done. Or hadn't done." As a quiet aside, she added, "Or was…or wasn't."

Dane groaned. "I'm sorry, Lacy. I sure never meant to have that kind of impact on you." He softly added, "Guess you're just one more person I let down."

Reaching out, she assuaged his obvious guilt as best she could with a light brush of her hand over his arm. The result was like electricity coursing between them. Sparking. Arching. Dancing.

Awkwardness plopped itself down between them then, but Lacy decided to ignore it as well as the pulsing current. She was determined to remain focused on the subject at hand.

"Don't feel too bad," she told him. "I got over you. I also got over that whole 'trying to be something I'm not' thing. By the time I'd entered my senior year of college, I'd decided that all men could just sit on their thumbs, for all I cared. I'm a nice person. Just the way I am. And if men can't see that, then to them, I say *pffft*." She made a rude noise with her tongue.

Dane chuckled. "I'm so glad you didn't lose your candor."

"Oh, for a while I did. My quiet stage, I called it." She rolled her eyes heavenward. "It was not a fun time to be me."

His smile widened, and Lacy felt her whole body flush with something dark and mysterious as heated tendrils curled low in her belly. She might not be able to put a name to whatever awe-inspiring thing it was that had trapped the two of them just moments before…but she could identify what was churning in her gut now.

Desire.

Hot. Vigorous. Insistent.

She wanted Dane Buchanan. And she wanted him bad.

"I can imagine," he quipped, teasing heavy in his tone. Without looking her way or slowing his stride, he added, "But, you know, that blunt outspokenness was one thing I always liked about you."

Lacy nearly gasped. "You did?"

"Uh-huh."

A chuckle bubbled from her throat before she had time to contain it. "That's funny. Most people—" what she'd wanted to say was most men "—find my, er...um—" she searched the air for a proper word "—*frankness* to be rather pushy, tactless and, yes, some have even labeled me with the horrible description of—" she gasped "—aggressive."

He stopped short then, swiveled his head her way and let his mouth drop open in mock horror. "How dare they?"

The laughter erupting from her was lighthearted. But as their gazes lingered, Lacy felt that amazing, awe-inspiring thing beginning to creep over them again.

Her laughter faded into oblivion. And the moment hung between them like a ripe, juicy piece of fruit just waiting to be plucked and savored. All they had to do was reach out for it. Wrap their fingers around it. She could almost taste the sweetness of his kiss on her tongue like sugary pear sap.

Suddenly, Dane seemed to force himself to face forward, a long stride carrying him away from her. He nickered to Jasper, tugging lightly on the animal's reins, and once again Lacy was forced to hurry to keep up with him.

"Would you slow down?" she called out to him. "My legs don't want to work right."

"Sorry." His voice was a mere murmur and he shortened his steps.

A distinct unease had slithered near, entwining itself between them. The magnetism—or whatever it was that had them both mystified and enthralled—really needed to be discussed. The thing felt so tangible, so lifelike, that it seemed intent on willing itself out into the open, forcing itself to be acknowledged...although she knew that thought was pretty ridiculous. However, she didn't quite know what to say. Or how to broach the subject when Dane was evidently content to pretend the strong attraction wasn't there.

Well, anything he could do, she could do better. Lacy could pretend just as well as he could.

The faint sounds of an engine disrupted the afternoon quiet. Dane slowed to a stop, lifting his gaze across the field. He was watching the horizon when the all-terrain-vehicle crested the rise to the east.

The boy riding the vehicle looked to be about fifteen. When he saw them, he applied the brakes. Just sat at the top of the hill.

Lacy got the distinct sense that the boy and Dane were facing off. There was definitely defiance in the boy's face. But there was something else, as well.

A neediness?

How silly, she thought. The teen was too far away for her to do anything more than imagine what he might be feeling.

However, she was close enough to Dane to get a clear sense of his reaction to the boy's appearance. His shoulder and neck muscles tensed, and he didn't take his eyes off the kid on the ATV.

Finally, the boy revved the engine and then shot back over the rise in the direction he'd come like a bullet blasted from a gun.

"That kid—"

The anger in Dane's tone made Lacy's eyes go wide.

"—is going to get himself hurt."

Curiosity welled up in her. But she didn't feel this was the best time to question Dane about the teen.

Seemingly out of nowhere, Alva's voice soughed through her mind.

Something happens to a man when memories and anxiety begin to poke at him. Anger is often the reaction you'll get, but fear is the driving force.

Lacy felt it was awfully odd that the advice Dane's father-in-law had imparted just that morning at the bridge would come skulking back into her thoughts at this moment. But the idea did lead her to wonder what on earth the belligerent-looking boy on the hill could have to do with the grief-stricken memories haunting Dane.

After supper that evening, Alva joined Dane and Lacy, and the three of them whiled away the evening on Dane's back porch sipping iced tea and talking about the day. Lacy had soaked in the tub while Dane had fried some chicken for their supper. And although her calves, thighs and rear end were still a little sore, she couldn't remember a time when she'd felt more relaxed.

Usually, her weekends were filled with running errands and paying bills, with laundry and housecleaning, with food shopping and all the other everyday responsibilities she didn't have time for during the week. She never got the opportunity to really unwind. Sitting outside watching the gray sky grow dark, she did just that.

Something about the country, the rolling hills that

rose to mountains in the not-too-far-off distance, the lush vegetation of the woods, the expanse of meadowlands, the wide-open spaces, just made one's worries dissolve.

Amazingly, Lacy Webs hadn't entered her head for hours and hours. As far as she knew, since starting her own business there hadn't been a minute when she hadn't worried about one thing or another: fretting over finances, planning new and interesting advertising, designing Web sites, researching new technology. She always seemed to be scheduling, arranging, working. Always working. It was so nice to simply sit. Gaze out at the mountains. Listen as Alva and Dane discussed cattle or chores or the beef market. Or just bask in the quiet when the conversation lulled.

Is this what life would be like if she were married to Dane? Each evening spent sharing and relaxing together? Maybe, a voice whispered from the back of her brain. But then the night would come. And relaxing would be the last thing on your mind...

Visions of hands and lips on smooth, naked skin flashed in her head, her senses bombarded with heat and longing—and a lust that was as delicious and pure and refreshing as springwater.

The imagery so startled her that she actually jerked, the ice in her tea tinkling against the sides of the glass.

Alva and Dane both stopped talking and turned to look at her.

"You've grown awfully quiet," Dane said. "What's on your mind?"

Making love with you. Feeling your fingers glide over my flesh. Kissing your mouth until we both can't breathe.

Even if Alva hadn't been present, none of those thoughts could have been uttered. Lacy knew that.

Her heart thudded and she felt overheated. Trapped into a corner by her own carnal desires. Her mind raced as she tried to think of something to say.

"That boy," she finally blurted. "The one we saw in the meadow today. I've been wondering who he is."

Relief flooded through her body and she took a calming breath. "Tell me about him."

"You saw Randy?" Alva asked his son-in-law.

Dane nodded. To Lacy, he said, "I've told that boy not to ride his ATV on our property. That thing upsets the cattle."

"Aw, now, Dane—" Alva's tone was cajoling "—Randy doesn't mean any harm. He's careful of our stock. He's only looking for—"

"He's looking to get himself hurt," Dane said. "He wasn't wearing a helmet. Again."

Alva looked over at Lacy. "Randy lives just down the road a ways. His mom and dad aren't home much. They're kinda famous around here. They have a television talk show. You may have heard of 'em. Liz and Tom Wilson from—"

"'The Wilson Hour,'" Lacy supplied. Her head bobbed and she smiled. "I have heard of them. Their Richmond talk show was on local cable and was just syndicated last year, wasn't it? I remember reading about it in the paper."

"It was," Dane answered. "And Randy's been on his own ever since."

Lacy frowned. "That's a shame."

"He's not a bad boy," Alva commented.

"He's a hooligan." Dane set down his glass on the

tile-topped side table. "And he's going to get himself into trouble. You mark my words."

"Let me get this straight," Lacy said. "The Wilsons leave their son alone out here in Oak Flat while they're in Richmond—"

"Oh, he's not all on his own," Alva rushed to correct her. "There's someone at the house all the time."

"But housekeepers, gardeners and limo drivers," Dane added, "can't substitute for parents. That boy needs to be disciplined by his mother and father."

The elderly man nodded his agreement. "Kids do need discipline. They crave it, in fact. Oh, children may think they want freedom. They might wish they didn't have any supervision at all, but the real truth is they feel safer when they have someone drawing the line for them, teaching them proper behavior." Alva chuckled, seeming to become lost in his thoughts. Then he said, "That way, kids can push the boundaries, and parents can shove them back. It's an age-old battle. It's how kids grow up knowing right from wrong."

All this talk of children and parents had Lacy's soul singing a silent song of yearning. She wished she knew what it felt like to hug a child, to scold a child, to love a child. Her chin tipped up as she shoved her way out of the sad reverie. She couldn't become lost in this poignant need right now. She just couldn't.

"When Randy comes around," Alva said, "I try to spend a little time with him. He's just looking for a role model, is all."

"The boy needs his parents." Dane picked up his tea and took a deep swallow.

"You sound as though you can't be bothered with

him." The opinion came tumbling from her lips before she had time to stop it.

"Yeah, Dane—" Alva's voice and eyes glittered with good-natured teasing "—we could have the little rascal arrested the next time he shows his face around here."

"All right, you two," Dane said, "I don't need this. I could go inside and be tortured by the evening news."

"Aw, now, we were only kidding," Alva told him.

But Lacy hadn't been joking. She'd called the situation just as she saw it. And something wouldn't allow her to let it go.

"If it's true what Alva said," she continued, "and the poor boy is only looking for a role model..."

Dane stood up then, rubbing his palms down the front of his thighs. "And I already told you—" he walked toward the back door as he spoke "—what the boy needs is supervision. From his parents."

Why was he being so stubborn about this?

She was surprised when he opened the screen. There was no mistaking the fact that he was intent on fleeing the scene.

"Well, his parents are never around," she couldn't help but point out, speaking loud enough so that even after he'd disappeared into the house she could be heard. "Maybe what he's looking for...maybe what he *needs*...is a friend."

Chapter Six

Through wind, rain, sleet and hail, time marches on. The weekend rolled into Monday, and Monday rolled into Tuesday. And although the storm had finally moved out of the area yesterday evening, the creek had not receded.

Lacy had kept in touch with her office each morning by phone. During that very first call, Lacy had explained that the bridge was probably safe to walk over but driving a car over it wasn't wise. Sharon had had offered to drive to Oak Flat to pick up Lacy and drive her back to Richmond.

"We can return for your car another day," Sharon had suggested. "Once that bridge is found safe enough to drive over. I wouldn't mind at all, you know."

Lacy had quickly but politely turned down the offer. She was having too much fun on this forced vacation.

However, Sharon had sensed something was up. "What are you scheming?"

"Scheming?" Lacy couldn't keep the injury out of her tone. "I am no schemer, Sharon."

The woman only laughed. "You can't fool me. Nothing short of finding a new client…or reaching some business goal would keep you from the office. So, what gives? What are you up to?"

Lacy had to laugh. "That was the old me. The new me is enjoying herself. She's riding horses. Watching the cattle graze. And sitting on the back porch watching the sun set."

Her assistant had chortled disbelievingly.

"The new Lacy is taking time to smell the roses. And she's spending some time becoming reacquainted with an old friend."

Since arriving in Oak Flat, she'd learned some things about life, and about herself. Life, she'd happily discovered, didn't have to be filled with work twenty-four hours a day, seven days a week. And she'd also learned that sometimes the troubles of others took precedence over your own.

But more importantly, she'd learned some things about Dane. He was harboring scars. He'd made comments that made her realize he was feeling wounded and bitter about the past. The wounds, she felt certain, had to do with losing his wife and daughter. But the bitterness had her stumped. His anger seemed to stem from some kind of self-reproach. For what, exactly, Lacy couldn't say. But these things did stir her curiosity.

And the way he seemed to shut out that young boy, the teenager who seemed to be looking for help…that confused Lacy. When she'd known Dane in college, he had a reputation of quickly and eagerly offering help to anyone who needed tutoring, or a shoulder to lean on. Lacy couldn't help but wonder if Dane's standoffish behavior toward the teenager named Randy might have something to do with the things that had happened in his past. But she hadn't been able to put all the pieces together to make any kind of coherent picture yet.

Of course, she didn't reveal all these things to Sharon.

"Just know," Sharon said, concern coating the words, "that I'm willing to come get you. Just give me a ring, and I can be there in a few hours."

"Thanks, Sharon. You're great. But I really am enjoying myself here."

And if I leave, a quiet voice echoed in her mind, *I won't be able to help Dane put the past behind him.*

That conversation had taken place yesterday. Her assistant had made the same offer this morning when Lacy called Richmond. And once again, Lacy turned down the chance to go home.

She hadn't yet found the perfect moment to talk to Dane about what was bothering him. But she would. Soon. Venting his grief would be healthy. And she wanted to offer him a shoulder to lean on.

There was something that the two of them had been dancing around. Skirting, really. Something that was making conversation awkward and stiff. And that something was the attraction that kept hounding the two of them. They both had become very conscious of it, and very self-conscious as a result.

The magnetism was impossible to deny. Just as it had forced its way between them on Saturday when they had gone riding together, this allure—this live, all-encompassing sexual chemistry—seemed to swirl and skitter and entangle itself around them whenever they were together.

And even when they weren't.

Lacy was having an awful time falling asleep at night. Knowing that Dane was only a hallway away…imagining him tangled in the sheets as he tossed and turned, sleepless and filled with need for her…mentally counting the few short steps it would take to be at his bedside, sliding beneath the cool sheets with him.

The misty, sexual visions her mind created made her anxious—no, they made her throb with desire for him. The carnal reflections made actually seeing him during the day all the harder. The need she felt pervaded her every thought, her every intention, her every word. She was afraid to approach him about anything. Mealtimes had become sheer torture. Lacy couldn't imagine attempting to talk to him about anything. Not when her desire was creating such agony within her.

What she needed was to steer clear of him today. What she needed was to remove him from her thoughts completely. What she needed was a long, brisk walk that would tax her body and free her mind of all the physical desire plaguing her.

Then, she'd be ready to face him. Then, she'd be prepared to coax him into telling all he had suffered. And why he wanted nothing to do with Randy. Surely, she'd persuade him to confide in her.

Alva caught sight of Lacy tramping across the meadow. The colorful flowers she carried in one hand were testament that she'd hiked through the patch of woods and up into the hill country. He and Dane both had wondered where she'd gone off to this morning.

She sure was a pretty little thing, he thought as he brought his truck to a stop in front of his house and cut the engine. And she'd been good for Dane.

Nothing was better for a man's soul than to be riled by a beautiful woman. The thought made him grin as he exited the truck, slamming the door shut behind him.

His son-in-law's eyes had glittered with such energy since Lacy's arrival. This woman had fired up Dane's anger. She'd made him throw his head back in carefree laughter. She'd made him think. And confused the hell out of him. She'd made the man come alive, she had. All in a matter of a few days.

There was something special between the two of them. Any fool could see that.

Dane might not want to realize it. But that was just because he wasn't ready. He was willing to blame his hot-and-bothered feelings on anything and everything but Lacy. And the way the two of them had been avoiding each other, Alva got the distinct impression that Lacy wasn't ready to recognize that special something, either.

Alva felt the need to do something about that. And the way things were panning out, he was going to have to do something sooner rather than later. Now that the bridge was safe, Lacy would be leaving. He couldn't allow that to happen.

"Hey, there!" Lacy called as she ran the last few yards between them. "You drove your truck over the bridge. I thought Dane said this morning that the water was still too high for him to get underneath there and look things over."

Nodding, the old man gave a shrug at the same time. "The water was high." The memory of Dane brought a grin to his face. "In fact, my son-in-law got a mite wet for his trouble." A chuckle escaped from deep in his chest. "And muddy, too. But he cleaned out the debris and checked the braces and beams. Everything looks okay."

Dane's rush to inspect the bridge was due to his wanting Lacy on her way back to Richmond. Oh, his son-in-law never actually said as much, but Alva suspected it. And he felt the need to do what he could to put a monkey wrench in the works.

He didn't want Lacy to leave. She was the best thing that had happened to Dane in years. Alva knew that...even if Dane didn't. Lacy was the first woman to get under Dane's skin...to get him all hot and bothered in...well, in a very long time.

Ever, Alva had to sadly admit.

Letting Lacy drive away would be a mistake. He had to do something.

He owed Dane. Owed him big. And what kind of man didn't repay his debts? No kind of man Alva wanted to be, that was for sure.

"So I guess you'll be leaving us this afternoon," Alva said.

A pensive expression took over Lacy's arresting features. Her eyebrows drew together and her blue eyes became cloudy.

"I guess," she said hesitantly. "But there was something I wanted to discuss with Dane before I left. I was hoping to do it tonight, after supper, when he was relaxed and...more receptive. But—"

The more she talked...the slower the words came...the cloudier her gaze got. He didn't know exactly what she was talking about, but whatever it was sure seemed important to her.

"—with the roadway clear, I guess I'll have to be on my way sooner than I thought…"

She wasn't too eager to get back to Richmond, that much was evident. Well, maybe Alva could do something to help her out with that problem.

A smile tugged at one corner of his mouth as a plan started to form in his mind. But he clamped his lips together tight. No sense in lettin' the whole world know the orneriness he was dreamin' up.

"Well, go on up and talk to him," Alva told her, shooing her with a wave of his hand. "I dropped him off at his house so he could have a shower. He's there now."

Her golden head bobbed, but when she turned and started toward Dane's house, Alva could see the spring was gone from her step. Well, he'd just have to see what he could do about that.

The shower was running when Lacy stepped through the back door. Dane's muddy clothing was in a heap beside the washer. It looked as if he'd come in and stripped right there in the laundry room. The idea of Dane prancing through the house bare-chested, in nothing more than his boxers, had Lacy nearly smiling.

Nearly. However, the overwhelming emotion she was dealing with kept her from doing so. She thought she was ready to talk with Dane…she thought she had planned the right words with which to convince him to confide in her. But she was still filled with trepidation just the same. No one liked to be told that they were living in the past and that it wasn't healthy.

With her mind focused on the conversation to come, she absently filled a glass with water and put the wildflowers she'd picked into it. Then she set the colorful bouquet in the middle of the kitchen table.

Dane had gone to such trouble to check that bridge, she realized. He'd gotten his jeans and shirt filthy, his boots were a mess, just so that she could get back to her business in Richmond as quickly as possible. He was so thoughtful. This was the considerate man she remembered from college.

The least she could do was tidy things up a bit.

She took the clothes out on the back porch and shook the worst of the mud off them. She loaded them into the washer, adding powder detergent and switching on the machine to run a small load. This mundane task was good for her. It helped to focus her thoughts.

This morning she'd walked across meadows and through a thick stand of pines and oaks, crossed a narrow stream and climbed up a steep sloping hill, all the while pondering what she wanted to say to Dane. When the sun had been high overhead, she'd turned back, thinking she still had plenty of time to prepare her consoling, helpful speech. She didn't want him thinking she felt he was utterly wretched in his holding onto his sorrow…or that he was wallowing in the past. She only wanted him to understand just how critical it was to let go.

When she'd met Alva a moment ago and discovered that the road back to Richmond was now clear and ready for her departure, she once again felt that horrible pressure of time. She needed a tranquil atmosphere in order to do justice to her feelings. She needed Dane to be calm and relaxed in order to really hear what she had to say. He'd be happier for it, she knew.

But here she was, racing the clock, she realized as she gazed out the window over the kitchen sink. She hated that feeling. Too much was riding on this for her to feel rushed.

The floorboards creaked behind her and Lacy turned, her heart clenching when she saw him, her blood thickening in her veins.

He stood in the doorway, a towel in one hand, a white T-shirt in the other, while something evidently intense occupied his mind, his full attention. His gaze was directed to a far corner of the room. She knew he hadn't seen her.

His feet were bare. The jeans he wore were clean, but well-worn, the soft and supple fabric a direct contradiction to the rock-hard muscular calves and thighs encased within. The metal stud closure rode just below his navel. Droplets of water still glistened in the springy hairs of his belly and chest.

He didn't realize he was being watched. That knowledge made her feel like a voyeur. But even so, she didn't look away. Didn't make a move. Or a sound. She couldn't take her eyes off him. Her pulse thundered through her, pounding against her eardrums, her temples, her throat. He had a magnificent body. Physical labor had made him hard. Solid. He had the kind of muscle and sinew that made a woman want to reach out, glide her fingers over the cords and ripples that lay just beneath his smooth, tanned skin.

That breathing, living *thing* was upon her again. And she was so overcome by the sheer magnitude of the allure dragging, luring, pulling, enticing, tugging at her that she felt woozy with it. It seized her.

Squeezed the breath out of her. Held her captive. But she knew without a doubt that she was a willing hostage.

The shirt made a slight rustling sound when he tossed it over the back of a chair. Then he lifted the towel, his biceps flexing, and rubbed the fluffy terry cloth over his hair.

He was going to see her, she realized, he was going to know she'd been watching him perform this most intimate act of drying himself. He was going to realize that she stood there, not saying anything, not alerting him to her presence, just staring.

But still she remained motionless, silent. Unable to force her gaze from him.

Just as she'd surmised, he lowered the towel, and his dark eyes swept the room, locking on her.

For the briefest of moments, surprise registered in his handsome face. But instantly he was as swept away by the hungry entity as she.

His corded throat convulsed when he swallowed, his eyes never leaving her face. The silence was awesome. And the walls seemed to close in on them, beckoning them closer, closer together. Lacy sensed all this, clearly saw that Dane sensed it, too, yet neither of them moved a single step.

After what seemed an hour, a week, a month, Dane tore his gaze from hers. He draped the towel over the chair back, snatched up his T-shirt and gathered the fabric in his hands. He pulled it over his head, stuffed his arms into the sleeves almost angrily, and then tugged the hem over his chest and belly.

Lacy would have been lying if she'd said she didn't feel deprived of the sight of him. But she forced her eyes to shift to the front of the refrigerator, studied the smooth surface without actually seeing it.

"The bridge is clear."

When he spoke, the fog dissipated. Oh, the thing that had zapped them, mesmerized them, wasn't completely gone. It had just been forced up into the corners of the room where it waited...waited. Lacy could feel it there, hovering, lingering...anticipating a vulnerable moment when it would once again ambush them.

"I know." Her voice sounded hoarse, dry. "I saw Alva outside. He told me."

"We couldn't find you."

"I went for a walk," she told him. "This morning at breakfast, you said you couldn't possibly get underneath the bridge until tomorrow..."

She remembered breakfast. Remembered the awkward stiffness that had enveloped them. Remembered how the air had throbbed and vibrated. Remembered how she hadn't been able to eat a thing because of it.

She added, "So I thought I had plenty of free time on my hands."

The real truth was, she couldn't imagine spending the day in the scorching heat. Heat that had absolutely nothing to do with the weather. She needed to be away from Dane. She needed to be in a place where she could collect her thoughts.

"Well, I finished up the morning chores early. And I knew how badly you wanted to be on your way."

Immediately, his gaze darted to the floor, and suspicion had the little hairs at the back of Lacy's neck standing on end. She didn't know why she should be wary of what he'd just said, why she would have needed to distrust his words, she only knew gut instinct had her feeling so.

"The weather's great," he continued, the words coming in a rush. "The sun is shining. It'll make for a pleasant drive back to Richmond." He picked up the towel, folded it this way, and then that.

Why would he act so fidgety? He was not the type of person to squirm.

"If you leave soon, you'll be home well before dinner."

He didn't look her in the face as he shifted from one foot to the other.

She was struck with a realization, and thoughts tumbled from her lips just as they formed in her head. "You didn't inspect the bridge for me. You didn't get all muddy so that I could get back to my business. You did it for you. You want me to leave. You want me back in Richmond. Out of your house. Out of your hair."

Although she hadn't meant to accuse him of anything, she knew there was plenty of finger-pointing in her tone.

He didn't dispute what she said. He couldn't. When he finally lifted those dark eyes to hers, she could see it plainly. She'd hit the bull right smack in the eye.

"It's for the best, Lacy." He reached up and combed his fingers through his damp hair. "You need to get back to Richmond."

What he really meant, she realized, was that he wanted her gone. What his eyes said was he *needed* her gone.

She couldn't believe it. Here she'd thought he'd gone to all this trouble, waded into all that creek, for her. She'd thought him considerate and thoughtful for doing so, too. But in reality he'd gotten himself all wet and mucky because he couldn't stand to have her in his home another night.

"Don't you think we ought to talk about this?" she said.

He frowned, and she realized that when she'd spoken the last word of her question, she'd pointed upward...to where the wall met the ceiling. Up there where she felt the *thing* was lurking, waiting.

But it wasn't up there, she realized in that instant. Her hand lowered of its own volition. The attraction, the amazing desire that plagued them wasn't hiding in the corners. It wasn't swirling near the ceiling. It was inside them. Inside them both.

Her palm splayed on her chest. Oh, how she wished she could rip out this allure she felt for Dane. How she wished she could toss it aside, throw it to the floor so she could be rid of it. How she wished she could drive away from Oak Flat, away from Dane without feeling as if her heart was going to be twisted and torn from her body.

Because that's exactly how she'd be feeling when she left. And so would he. She knew it just as surely as she knew the sun was shining in the sky outside.

"What I think," he said, his soft voice seeming in direct contrast to the vehemence of his thoughts on the matter, "is that talking about it would be futile."

At least he wasn't denying that there was something to talk about.

Lacy's chin tipped up. "You wouldn't talk about what we were feeling for each other twenty years ago, Dane. Whether that was because of that plan you said you had or because of Helen, I don't know for certain. But our not talking about it back then affected me. It *wounded* me, Dane. For a very long time. Back then I was in awe of you. I'd have done anything you said. I avoided talking about what was between us because you intimated that we should. I followed your lead. I didn't mention it. Didn't raise the subject. But I'm all grown-up now. I'm not easily awed anymore.''

His jaw tensed, but he said nothing.

''I'm attracted to you, Dane,'' she blurted. ''And you're attracted to me.'' A frown bit into his forehead. ''Although—'' she shook her head ''—attraction just doesn't describe…just isn't big enough to express what's between us. We *want* each other. We're *drawn* to each other. You know it. And so do I. How can you not want to talk about it? How can you not want to…to *explore* it?''

Fire glistened in his grey eyes now.

''You think I don't want to explore this…this—'' Frustration tightened the corners of his mouth as he hunted his brain for the right words. *''—whatever it is we're feeling?''*

Evidently, he, too, was of the opinion that attraction was a wholly inadequate description.

''Don't you think I want to give in to the urge to touch you, to hug you, to kiss you, to hold you?''

All those things sounded like paradise to Lacy. If only he would act on any of those urges. She'd felt those desires herself. Powerfully. Forcefully. Even though she had known he'd experienced the same allure as she, it was freeing to hear him actually say the words.

He'd felt it twenty years ago, and he felt it now.

But twenty years ago, he'd refused to acknowledge their feelings for each other. Now, she refused to allow him to ignore them.

The song in her soul became louder with each passing second.

She took a single step toward him.

"Don't."

He hadn't raised his voice, but the tiny word stopped her in her tracks.

"But...but *why?*" Her question encompassed a full spectrum of confusing issues.

Why didn't he want to talk about this? Why did he feel that expressing themselves about their emotions was useless? Why didn't he want to explore these wonderful, amazing feelings coursing though them? Why was he continuing to ignore the huge, hungry, yearning beast that was just behind them, above them, all around them? Why wouldn't he just let them be devoured by it? Why wouldn't he hold her? Touch her? Kiss her? *Why?*

As if he was cognizant of every question rolling through her mind, he said, "I just can't, Lacy. I can't do it."

All traces of sternness and anger dissolved from his face then. His shoulders sagged and he sighed. He rubbed a hand over his jaw.

She couldn't bring herself to repeat her question, so she simply remained silent.

When he lifted his gaze to hers once more, he looked drained. As if fighting this battle had taken a great deal out of him.

"I cannot take the chance of disappointing another person in my life."

His voice was a mere whisper that triggered chills to course across her skin. Without thought, she crossed her arms over her chest in an attempt to hug away the frosty apprehension that had fallen over her shoulders.

"I don't want to disillusion anyone else. I don't want to fail any more people in my life."

"But how can you disappoint me?" she asked. "I'm not asking anything of you. I'm not asking any more than that you…allow us to…"

She let the rest of the sentence trail off as she watched his expression harden, saw him shake his head.

"It's impossible. Trust me. I can't offer you any explanations. I'm not going to go into it. Just know that I'm doing what's best. For both of us."

But he needed to go into it. He needed to confide all the hurt and grief he felt. He needed to lean on someone. He needed to let it out. Let it go. So he could be free of it. So he could live a normal life. Find happiness. Contentment. Love.

As it was, she suspected there was too much dark emotion cluttering up his mind. He simply had to release it.

"What you need to do is go pack your bag," he continued. "You need to get into your car and drive back to Richmond. Right now. This minute."

But this minute, packing her things and leaving was the last thing on her mind.

"Okay, okay," she found herself saying as she rummaged through her thoughts for all those perfect words she'd so carefully planned to say to him. "Hold on, though. Just a second."

She'd meant to talk him into entrusting her with his feelings, with all his bad memories of the past.

"Before I go," she said, "I have something I want to talk about. Something I want to say to you."

From the look on his face, he really didn't want to hear anything she had to say. He only wanted her gone so his life could return to normal.

But he was wasting away here. Working from sun-up to sundown. Rarely going off the spread. Never socializing. What kind of life was that?

Finally, she got up the nerve to say, "You need to let go of your grief."

"Lacy."

He didn't want her help. The tone of his voice told her so.

"I can't talk about this, honey."

"Let me be your friend, Dane. I want to help you."

"I know you do. But what you need to understand is that no one can help me." Stressing his point, he repeated, "No one."

"But if you'd just talk about it—"

He cut off with a shake of his head.

The rejection that walloped her was more devastating than she'd ever imagined. She'd offered him her hand. Offered him her shoulder. Her friendship. And he'd refused her.

Her spine straightened. "Well, then." She took a deep breath. "I guess there's nothing left to be said. I'll go pack my things and be on my way."

She felt numb when she walked past him. She felt numb as she stuffed her business suit into the over-night bag. She even felt numb when she gathered her purse and keys.

Numbness was good. Very good. It would get her home in one piece.

However, that wonderful anesthetized feeling didn't last long. When she got into her car, turned the key in the ignition and nothing happened, frustration exploded inside her—a frustration that had her pounding the steering wheel and uttering a most unladylike curse.

Chapter Seven

Lacy thanked her lucky stars when Alva happened upon her so quickly after she discovered that her car wouldn't start. He'd popped open the hood, tinkered with the engine, and then left her sitting in the shade of Dane's porch while he drove his truck to the automotive store.

The elderly man was a lifesaver. He'd happily and graciously offered to fix her car when he returned. Alva was a shining example of a fine southern gentleman, not like some other people Lacy knew.

She shoved the dark thoughts of Dane from her mind.

Lacy hadn't wanted to remain behind, but when she'd eagerly suggested she accompany Alva to the store, he'd explained that he had an errand or two of his own that needed running…errands, she'd guessed from his unspoken insinuation, that needed a bit of privacy. So she'd found shelter from the hot afternoon sun by sitting in the shade of Dane's front porch. And that's where he found her just after Alva had driven off.

"Car trouble?"

"Don't you worry," she told him, her clipped tone the result of her overwhelming hurt knowing he had refused all that she had offered him. "It's just a dead battery. Your father-in-law was kind enough to offer to go after another one for me. As soon as he gets back, I'll be out of your hair."

"Why didn't he just give you a jump start? That battery must have been in pretty bad shape." After a moment, Dane said, "Well, come on inside. You can wait where it's cool."

"No thank you. I'm fine right here."

She looked out over the horizon, watched the cattle that dotted the landscape. She heard him sigh.

"Come on, Lacy," he said quietly. "Don't sulk. Come inside. He's going to be gone a while."

"Sulk?" Her back went rigid. She should have asked what he'd meant when he said Alva would be gone a while, but she was too busy feeling insulted. "I'll have you know I have never sulked in my life."

His chuckle was soft, and with it he clearly communicated that he disagreed with her. As glares go, she was proud of the one she speared him with. But he didn't seem the least bit affected by it.

"If you're not sulking," he continued with undisguised humor in his voice, "do you mind telling me why your shoulders are as tight as an overcoiled spring and your mouth is puckered up like you just sunk your teeth into a plump, juicy lemon?"

She looked at him a moment. She hated to admit he was right. But she *was* sulking.

Lacy released the tension that had built up in her

body. Inhaling deeply, she tucked her top lip between her teeth and glanced down at her scuffed and dusty canvas sneakers. She exhaled slowly.

She wasn't being fair to Dane.

If he couldn't bring himself to talk about his pain, he couldn't do it. There was no forcing it.

She had never been widowed. Had never lost a child. She probably couldn't even imagine the anguish he'd experienced.

She forced her gaze to lift to his.

"You're right," she confessed. "I have been sitting here sulking. And it hasn't been very mature of me." She stood up. "I'll wait for Alva inside where it's cool."

She followed him into the house, very aware—and also distressed—that the warm, male scent that was his alone made her belly churn with tight little fireworks. Desire spiraled inside her and she tried hard to tamp it down. But it wasn't the kind of fire that was easily snuffed out.

"What did you mean?" she asked, determined to ignore the heat growing inside her. "When you said Alva would be a while."

"Oak Flat doesn't have an automotive store. He'll have to drive to the next town. It'll take him an hour or so to get back."

Silently, she remembered the errands Alva said he had to run, and then she wondered just how long he might take to return with the battery.

"You didn't have any lunch," he told her. "And it's nearly time for dinner. How about a bite to eat?"

She smiled, grateful for anything that would take her mind off the awful yearning he caused in her.

"Now that you mention it, I'm starved. What's on the menu?"

"I put some spaghetti sauce in the Crock-Pot this morning," he said. "All we have to do is boil some water for pasta and toss us up a quick salad."

Three hours later, Alva still hadn't returned. Dane and Lacy had eaten dinner and cleaned up the mess. They had watched the evening news, and when the first nightly game show appeared on the TV screen, Dane had snapped off the television and suggested that, since the evening had surely cooled off, they sit out on the back porch and enjoy the night.

Tension hovered around them. She realized he felt guilty, because of the oh-so-gentle way he was treating her. As if he thought she were made of delicate bone china.

They stared at the salmon-streaked sky. One thing was certain, she thought: sunsets in this part of Virginia were more beautiful than she'd ever seen anywhere else.

Quite out of the blue, a huge sigh issued from him. He laced his fingers together, tucked them under his chin, and as he gazed out at the tranquil scenery, he said, "My father was disappointed in me."

There was something heart-wrenching in the way he said those words…so agonizingly heart-wrenching that Lacy felt suddenly frantic in her need to lighten his mood.

"So was mine," she said, hoping to make him understand that she really could relate. She remembered when she'd first arrived how Dane had asked about her baseball-card collection and how she'd said that hobby was her only link with her son-craving father, the thin thread that had connected them.

Without taking his eyes off the horizon, Dane said, "Did your father ever threaten to disown you? Mine did."

"Oh, now," she said. "Parents go off the deep end every now and then. Your dad might have been momentarily irritated by—"

"He meant to do it, too. I failed him. Terribly. Went against everything he believed in."

Lacy realized that Dane hadn't even heard her attempt to mitigate the situation he was describing.

"And if he hadn't gotten sick…if he hadn't died," he continued, "he'd have gone through with it. I saw the papers. If he'd been able to sign them, he'd have taken away my share of the business. He'd have handed it over to Alva."

"I can't believe that." Lacy whispered the words, an ache squeezing at the very heart of her. "But why? Why would he do such a thing? Fathers are supposed to love their children. Provide for them. Bolster them up. Make them feel secure, cared for, adored."

The statements, she suddenly realized, were made for her own benefit as well as Dane's. So many times over the years she'd wondered what she could have done, what she could have said, what mountain she could have climbed, to have captured her father's attention, garnered his love.

Eric Rivers had been a cool, quiet man. A man who had found it impossible to express his thoughts and emotions. And Lacy had often questioned her mother as to why he kept his distance from her.

"He's got a lot on his mind," her mother would say. Or she'd explain, "He's a busy man." Or she'd defend him with, "He's just the quiet sort, Lacy. Leave him be."

It hadn't just been his silence that had given Lacy the idea that her father hadn't wanted anything to do with her. It was also the fact that he'd ignored her through most of her adolescence and young adulthood. No matter how hard she tried, how many excellent report cards she'd brought home, how many successes she'd achieved in her early career, she couldn't remember a single instance where her father had told her he'd been proud of her. Even as he lay dying, he'd been unable to express his feelings.

Lacy shook the fog of the past from her brain and focused on the here and now. Dane was talking about his relationship with his own father. She didn't need to get caught up in her own sorrows.

She repeated, "Why, Dane? Why would he do such a thing?"

Another sigh rushed from deep in his chest. "Bud Buchanan was always a bitter man. A hard man. I knew that. Lived with it every day. I became a master at discerning the signs. Knowing when I should disappear and when it was okay to emerge from the shadows. Alva and Helen did their best to protect me." He murmured, "They protected me as well as they could, and I'll be forever grateful."

He went quiet. But Lacy knew he'd need no more prompting from her. He'd begun this journey into the past. He'd finish in his own good time. What she needed now was patience.

"You see," he finally continued, "my mother left us. She didn't say why. We just woke up one day and she was gone. She never contacted us. And we never knew where she went.'' Then he added, ''My father blamed me.''

Dane looked at her then, connected with her, and the intensity in his deep gray eyes nearly stole her breath away.

''I was so young when she left that I don't even remember what she looked like. Don't remember the color of her eyes. The shape of her face. The color of her hair.''

Hot tears sprang to Lacy's eyes in reaction to the agony he was carrying on his shoulders. His pain was immense. The weight of it was great. So great. Overwhelming. And it seemed he had carried it for a long, long time.

Why on earth would a father place such a heavy load on a little boy?

The question haunted Lacy because she knew now was not the time to satiate her curiosity...now was the time to listen.

His gaze latched onto the horizon once again, his fists jammed under his chin. ''I was able to see my mother one last time,'' he said. ''When I was nine, Alva found me in the barn, put me in the car and we drove away from here without a word to my father who was out with the stock. Alva drove for what seemed like hours until we got to Richmond. To a dirty, run-down part of the city. I was scared. Too scared to ask any questions. We found this lady...Alva said it was my mother...lying unconscious on a bed made up in filthy linens.''

He rubbed a shaky hand over his mouth. ''We got her to a hospital, but she never regained consciousness. I was furious. So angry that she'd left me, and only called for me when it was too late.''

The sigh he heaved was sharp, and Lacy suspected that, even after all these years, he still harbored some of that anger against his mother.

"When we returned home," Dane continued, "Dad gave me a beating. For leaving without saying anything. For betraying him by going to see my ma. Alva tried to intervene, but my dad socked him right in the jaw. Dad was so shocked he'd hit Alva, he forgot all about punishing me. The next day, he acted as if the whole thing hadn't happened. And we never mentioned my mother again."

His tongue smoothed over his lips. "I already told you my dad was hard. And he wanted me to be hard, too. He thought that was the best way to survive. You see, he was a cattleman, through and through, my dad was. And he was raising me to be a cattleman, too. Oh, we had plenty of good times. There was nothing else like working with him in the wide-open spaces. He was good at what he did. Knew the cattle business inside and out. And he believed that everything I needed to know could be learned right here on this little patch of earth. And he was right, I guess."

His voice took on a far-off quality as he added, "But there was a spirit in me. A spirit that wanted to spread its wings. A spirit that wanted to experience things. See things. Learn things. Things I couldn't experience and see and learn at home."

It seemed to Lacy that Dane was justifying his behavior, his actions, to himself if to no one else, as if he'd justified to himself many times.

"It's not like I wanted to travel the world," he said. "All I wanted was a college education. And I was a pretty good high-school student."

Lacy dashed away an errant tear, unable to quell

her smile, remembering the many stimulating conversations they'd had in the college library, remembering how she'd admired his intelligence, remembering his National Honor Society status. He hadn't merely been a pretty good student all those years ago. He'd been an exceptional student. An exceptional young man.

"A counselor from high school told me I could probably get myself an academic scholarship to college," Dane said. "But even a free ride wouldn't persuade my dad. He was against my going. Even though I assured him that my plan was to finish school and come right back home to work the spread, he was still dead set against the idea."

So that was the plan he'd so firmly followed all those years ago. The one that kept him from dating her. But it didn't make sense to her, she realized. She'd been so mindlessly crazy over him back then, she'd have followed him anywhere. To Oak Flat or New York City or Timbuktu.

Again, he grew quiet. Patience, Lacy told herself. Patience. A quiet voice inside her head told her that soon all her questions would be answered.

"But Helen pushed me to pursue an education. She'd been sweet on me for longer than I could remember. All she could see was what she thought was best for me. The two of us had grown up together, you see. I'd always been fond of her, always cared about her, but..." He let the rest of the thought die away. "When I dragged my heels, she got her daddy to start nagging me, too."

His mouth pulled back, a sad, shadowy smile tugging at its corners.

"I wanted to go so bad." The sigh that flowed from

him was small and tight. "So bad." He swallowed. "I finally did it. I went against my father's wishes. I filled out the college application. Sent in a transcript of my grades. Wrote a killer essay. Jumped through all the hoops the entry board held up. And I went to college. On a full scholarship. I was sure that once I'd finished, once I'd returned home and Dad saw that I meant to stay and work the spread with him, things between us would get better."

Again, their gazes touched. Bonded.

"Midway through my sophomore year, my dad got sick. Had a stroke that left him partially paralyzed. I was sure I'd have to give up on my education. Come home and help out with the business. But Alva and Helen refused to let me give up on my dream of earning my degree. They cared for my dad all those months I was away. Alva helped him bathe himself. Helped him get dressed every morning. Helen came to the house and cooked for him. Cleaned the house. Washed his clothes. And every time he got into one of his moods, every time he started ranting that I should come home where I belonged, she stood right up to him. She told him he should want me to better myself. Educate myself."

He laughed softly.

"Many a time, she made him feel so low that he'd back down." His handsome profile softened. "You've got to understand about Helen. She was a delicate little thing. She had cerebral palsy. The disease didn't affect her intelligence, but it did impinge on her posture and her gait." He solemnly added, "And her spirit. She didn't like leaving the property. Even to go into Oak Flat. This place was her life. Her handicap practically imprisoned her here. It left her feeling self-conscious. Completely demolished her confidence.'' Another ghostlike smile hovered on his lips. ''But when it came to taking up for me, she'd turn into a lioness.''

His tone hardened, his jaw turning to granite.

''Like I said, she often had Dad backing down. But lots of times she rushed home crying. Especially after I'd left for college and wasn't around to stop her from confronting him. She never told me he upset her...but Dad bragged about it when I was home on summer breaks. Often.'' His dark head shook. ''I'll never forgive him for treating her badly.''

Bragged about it?

Lacy didn't know what to say. She was overwhelmed by all she was learning. Dane's wife had had to deal with the physical limitations of a debilitating disease. His father had blamed him for his mother's leaving, had been verbally and mentally abusive, and the man hadn't wanted his son to attend college.

To think that she'd known Dane all those years ago, cared deeply for him, yet she never knew about all the turmoil he was experiencing in his personal life...with his father.

Up until this moment, she had thought her own childhood had been bad. Compared to Dane's, her upbringing had been a picnic. Her father might not have showed her any physical signs of love, but he had provided her with shelter and sustenance and clothing, and he hadn't made a game of ripping apart the self-esteem of those around him, as Dane's father seemed to have done.

She wanted to reach out to Dane. To touch him. Comfort him. To somehow take away the pain that was locked in all those memories in his head. But she knew he wasn't finished.

"During my last year at the university," he continued quietly, "just after I'd met you, my dad had a second stroke. A massive one that left him completely paralyzed. He wasn't able to do anything for himself. He needed twenty-four-hour-a-day care."

His profile grew pinched with the painful memories.

"Alva called me and I came right home. Dad couldn't speak, but I could see the anger smoldering in his eyes when he looked at me. I could feel him pointing blame at me even though he couldn't lift a finger." He inhaled deeply. Exhaled soulfully. "I failed my father. And what I discovered later…after his death…was that he'd begun the process of disinheriting me. He'd had the papers in his possession for a while. If he'd been able to sign them, or even communicate to the lawyers that cutting me out of his will was his true and final decision, he'd have done it."

How could anyone be so mean-spirited? Lacy wondered. To use and abuse the people in his life like that. To blame others for the bad things that happened to him. It probably wasn't very nice of Lacy to think so, but she was glad she'd never met the callous, nasty man.

"After his second stroke," Dane continued, "I had every intention of staying with him. But Helen and Alva would have none of that. I was too close to finishing, they said. Too close to reaching my dream."

Dane stretched his neck first one way then the

other. Then he rolled his shoulders. Talking about the past evidently had him tense, his muscles overtaxed.

"Helen and I had an argument. She was certain I should go back, and I was just as certain that I should stay. The lioness came out in her. I'd never seen her so angry. She argued from every angle imaginable, but I held my ground. I needed to be at home. Finally, she began to cry."

Even in the waning twilight, Lacy saw his eyes grow misty. These recollections were private. Too intimate for her to feel comfortable with. However, despite her uneasiness, she sensed that it was important to Dane to get this out.

"She told me that all she'd ever lived for was my happiness. And that's when I realized just how deeply she'd loved me all those years. I'd cared about her, of course. And I'd teased her about being sweet on me. But to her—"

His words broke off as he was forced to swallow around the emotion that lodged in his throat. Lacy felt her chin tremble.

"To her," he repeated, "it was no joke. She said that fate had made it impossible for her to live a normal life. That she was living vicariously through me. And that it was her greatest wish for me to live my dream. Attain my goal. To earn my degree."

Dane turned to face Lacy now. And the overwhelming sentiment registered on his handsome face made her tears well and fall unheeded down her cheeks.

"It was at that moment that I realized," he said, "just how much I owed Helen. She loved me. More than my mother ever had. More than my father had, too. All she'd ever wanted was for me to be happy."

He surveyed the wooden planks of the porch floor, then lifted his gaze to Lacy's. "My heart had never been so filled with gratitude as at that moment. And even though I had met you...even though I had felt strong stirrings of attraction for you, I desperately wanted to offer Helen something for all she'd sacrificed for me. For all that fate had stolen from her. So I decided to do what I could to give her a normal life. I asked her to marry me."

His lips pursed, and again he swallowed. "She deserved a little happiness for all she'd done."

Lacy's throat ached with emotion. The fallible, very human part of her wanted to shout, but what about *me?* What about *us?* But the questions quickly faded into oblivion when she tried to imagine the isolation and insecurities Helen had suffered in her young life, all the young woman had endured while caring for the hateful Bud Buchanan so that the man she loved could have the chance to reach for his dream, and Lacy knew without a single doubt that Dane had done the right thing.

It was then that she realized she could keep silent no longer. "She did, Dane. She deserved all the happiness you could give her."

Some of the tension dissolved from Dane's face then. He actually looked relieved that she'd agreed with him.

"She accepted my proposal," he said. "And I went back to school. My dad had nurses coming and going. He had Alva and Helen. And my being here wasn't going to change his condition. So I went back to take my final exams and earn my degree."

Disgust cast a pall over the planes and angles of his face. "After that article came out...the one with all that perfect-man nonsense—'' he shook his head, his mouth twisting derisively ''—Helen refused to marry me. She said I deserved someone else. Someone healthy. Someone tall, statuesque, graceful.'' His voice lowered as he added, ''Someone beautiful.''

He rubbed his fingers over his chin. ''But I told her she was beautiful. And that I wanted her for my wife.'' His intense gaze zeroed in on Lacy. ''Helen's body may have been bent and twisted, and she might have had some muscular spasms when she walked, but she was beautiful. On the inside…and on the outside.''

''From all that you've said,'' Lacy easily admitted, ''your wife was a wonderful person. A woman with a big heart.''

''She almost wasn't my wife. We argued about getting married for six months. I kept telling her over and over that she was who I wanted. She was good. And kind. And caring. And giving. She was just the person I wanted to spend my life with.''

Although she hated herself for noticing, Lacy couldn't help but be aware of the fact that not once had he ever used the word *love* in describing his feelings for Helen, in his arguments for persuading the woman to marry him. Oh, he'd said she had loved him, had sacrificed for him, had wanted nothing but his happiness. But the strongest word he'd used to describe his own feelings had been to say he'd been fond of her, that he'd cared about her, that he'd been grateful for all she'd done for him.

Still, Lacy decided, in a world filled with quick marriages based on shallow, fleeting feelings and speedy, painful divorces, all the emotions Dane mentioned could make for a strong foundation on which to build a relationship. Their marriage would have had a great chance of seeing a long future, had Helen lived.

"The important thing is," Lacy pointed out, "you succeeded in making her happy. You married her. You and she had a beautiful daughter together."

She'd hoped to make him smile, and he didn't disappoint her. Lacy's heart quickened at the sight of it.

"Helen was so happy when she realized she was pregnant with Angel," Dane said. "We'd been married more than ten years before Helen became pregnant. We'd gone through so much. My dad had died. And I realized that the business wasn't in very good financial shape. My father's illness had taken an economic toll on the bottom line. We worked hard to build it back up, Alva and Helen and I. Then…like a gift from above, Angel came into our lives. We were in heaven. All of us."

His blissful tone was short-lived.

"But in the end, I failed Helen and Angel even worse than I failed my father."

The hard edge in his voice appeared seemingly out of nowhere and it left Lacy feeling suddenly anxious.

"It was my fault that Helen and Angel drowned in the creek that afternoon," he said. "So many times over the years I'd hotdogged it over that bridge when high water was swirling and churning over the passageway. I'd acted recklessly so many times, a few times with Helen in the truck with me."

Regret thickened his throat, seeming to make it difficult for him to speak. His eyes misted with guilt and deep remorse, and Lacy felt her own eyelids burning with tears.

"She'd had Angel to the doctor. Usually, I took

them into town. But it was calving season. And we had several difficult births all happening at once. Neither Alva nor I could leave. So Helen went on her own. All she could think about was getting the baby some medicine…and then high-tailing it back home. She hated being off the spread. I knew that. I felt so helpless. It was pouring rain. And when she tried to return—''

His voice broke then, and he went quiet. Evidently he could speak no more.

The silence swelled. Churned. And she thought her heart was going to break in two. In that instant, she realized just what this man meant to her. What he'd *always* meant to her, even though they had been separated by twenty years of living.

She loved him. Had never stopped loving him in all this time.

It was clear that he felt he'd made some mistakes. He felt he'd failed those he loved the most. But for the life of her, Lacy couldn't agree.

After hearing his story, she knew in her heart that he'd only done the best he could do. He thought he was flawed. Imperfect. But Lacy knew the truth.

He was better than perfect.

He'd ignored his own desires all those years ago in order to do right by a woman who had given him so much. It was a tragedy, a horrible accident that had taken Helen and Angel from him.

He needed to know that. He needed someone to tell him.

With no other thought in her mind, Lacy was on her feet, moving toward him, squatting between his knees, gazing gently up into his tortured eyes, placing her palms on his warm, hard thighs. Her only thought was to offer him comfort. Her only thought was to take away some of the enormous pain that fairly pulsed from him. Her only thought was to soothe. Assure. Console.

Chapter Eight

He hadn't meant to dredge up the past. Doing so was perilous for him. Opening the door on those memories of how he'd failed his father. Remembering the circumstances surrounding the death of his wife and daughter. These thoughts never failed to churn up a long list of torturous "should haves" that haunted him. It would take him days and days to set the regret and guilt aside so that he could function in a normal manner.

But Lacy had pushed him. She'd stood before him this afternoon and urged him to talk about his pain.

He'd avoided revealing the past to Lacy. Avoided talking about the past twenty years like they had been the black plague. He hadn't wanted her to know how inadequate he had been as a son, a husband and a father. Hadn't wanted her to realize how he'd failed those he loved. However, once he'd started talking, it was as if the floodgates had opened. There had been no stopping the deluge.

A strange sadness filled him now. But he was relieved as well. For now Lacy would understand him fully. She'd comprehend all the reasons why he'd refused to father her child. She'd easily figure out why he continued to ignore the attraction they felt for one another.

Because he simply could not risk failing another living soul.

Dane hadn't even been aware that Lacy had moved until he felt the heat of her palms on his thighs. He dragged his gaze from the twilit horizon.

Shadows partially obscured her delicate features, but the immense compassion expressed in her glistening, azure eyes was like a punch to his gut. Every muscle in his body tensed. *Every muscle.* Feverish waves coursed through him, emanating from deep inside, tumbling, twirling, spiraling.

That all-consuming *thing* was upon him again. That thing he couldn't put a name to. Attraction. Fascination. Magnetism. None of these words quite described what had plagued him so terribly ever since Lacy had reentered his life.

Desire?

Well, yes. Of course. But even this strong designation didn't fully express all the emotions that twisted and curled inside him as he gazed at Lacy. Hell…he reacted in this manner when he no more than thought of the woman.

Love.

The word tore through his mind as if it had been an arrow shot from a bow.

No, his mind screamed at him. He couldn't love Lacy. He wouldn't let himself!

Distance. He needed distance. And he needed it now.

He felt the overwhelming need to communicate this thought to her. She shouldn't be so close to him. It was unsafe for him. For them both.

Dane didn't know if he actually verbalized her name, or if he'd merely mouthed it. But before he even had a chance to draw breath, she was on her knees, reaching for him, pulling him into a tight embrace.

"It's okay," she murmured. "I'm not asking for anything. I just have this overwhelming urge to…I think you need…"

She smelled so good. Exotic. Enticing. Like flowers and rain, like warm honey, like…

Lacy.

He didn't reach for her. Didn't move. Didn't lift his hands or his arms. However, he did close his eyes, and he felt himself moving closer and closer to the edge of some dark and mysterious precipice.

Dig in your heels, logic shouted. Don't allow yourself to go any closer.

She said, "You need a hug, Dane. You need a little comfort."

And he was lost.

He fell, plunging, tumbling, crashing headlong over the cliff and into the secretive and shadowy depths that had been beckoning him ever since Lacy's arrival. He smoothed his hands up her back, splayed them there, pulled her against him, buried his face in her neck, breathed in the sweet, sensuous, womanly scent of her.

Her breasts pressed tightly against his chest, her long nails lightly raking the tender skin at the back of his neck. Her fingers combed into his hair and she softly massaged his scalp in tiny back-and-forth movements. The smell of her, the feel of her in his arms, her touch on his skin made him grow rock-hard.

Ever so fleetingly, he wondered where the jumble of awful emotion had gone. Where was his grief? His guilt? His sorrow and regret? Where were all those bad feelings he knew would stick close for days on end?

But just as soon as the questions whispered through his head, they dissolved into nothing, leaving behind only the hot and pulsing need…the fiery yearning that threatened to burn him alive.

He dragged her from him, cradled her lovely, delicate face between his rough hands, and he couldn't help but notice the stark contrast between their coloring. He, with his sandpapery fingertips and palms and sun-baked skin, she with her creamy cheeks and golden hair and eyes like bright, glittering sapphires. She was as beautiful as a princess. Regal as a queen. Graceful as an angel. He had no business wanting her, touching her. But, heaven help him, he *did* want her. And he *would* touch her.

Her skin was like silk as he ran the pads of his fingers over her cheekbone. The rapid pulse he detected at her temple made his own heart beat erratically. Her hair was downy soft and he weaved his fingers deep into the short, silky tresses.

The compassion he'd seen in her blue, blue eyes had metamorphosed into…

Dane's breath went dead in his throat when he saw everything he, himself, was feeling—all the needful aching, the awesome hunger, the passionate craving— reflected in the warm, limpid pools of her eyes.

She wanted him just as much as he wanted her.

In that instant, he knew if he didn't taste her sweet lips he was going to completely lose his hold on sanity. He stared into her face, his eyes silently pleading for permission. She didn't verbalize her consent. She did better than that. She lifted her chin, offering him her luscious, yielding mouth. And he covered it with his own.

Nectar. Sweet as syrup. Hot as fire. Moist. Delicious. Succulent as ripe fruit warmed by the summer sun.

When he'd kissed her twenty years ago, he remembered thinking how delectable she'd tasted. As he kissed her now, it was as if no time at all had passed.

He wrapped his arms around her waist, and in one fluid motion, he stood, bringing her with him, all the while nibbling, nipping, tasting her sumptuous lips.

Her throat was hot against his mouth, and with each beat of her heart, he felt a pulsation against his tongue. He sucked, his mouth open, his teeth ever so gently abrading her heated flesh, and he was rewarded with a deep, soulful moan that vibrated from deep down inside her. The need that throbbed through him quickened, intensified.

His name rolling from her lips sounded raw, erotic to his ears, and he had no clue what was keeping his knees from buckling from underneath him. He felt quaky with desire.

His hand slid around her body until the fullness of her breast lay heavy in his palm. Unwittingly, his thumb roved over her nipple and it budded into a hard nub. She gasped with pleasure, and joy surged through him.

The fabric of her T-shirt was thin, but he wanted

it gone. Wanted to see her body. Wanted to devour her with his eyes. With his hands. With his tongue. Wanted to see and touch and taste the dusky nipples he'd been forced to only imagine…and dream about. Until now.

Impatiently, he tugged at the fabric of her shirt where it was tucked into the waistline of her jeans. The atoms in the air seemed to speed up, grow wild. Frantic. The sound of their breathing did, too.

Her feathery kisses touched his lips, his cheeks, his nose, his chin, all the while she helped him gather up the cotton of her top. The pale rose-hued satin of her bra came into view, and Dane felt as giddy as a randy teen on his first date. His mouth went so dry that his throat felt painful when he tried to swallow. Two more seconds and her body would be in plain sight. His heart thundered like the hooves of a horse, his blood turned to molten lava—

''Dane?''

Alva's voice shocked him. Evidently, it shocked Lacy, too, for she sprung away from him, hastily tucking the hem of her shirt back into her jeans.

''You back here?''

His father-in-law rounded the corner of the house just as Lacy plopped herself down in a chair, pressing her slender fingertips to her still-moist lips, her eyes wide with distress.

''Yeah, Alva,'' Dane said, straining to rise from the sensuous fog enveloping him. ''We're back here watching the sun set.''

The elderly man chuckled. ''Well, since you haven't noticed, the sun went down a while ago.''

He felt his face flame and was glad that the evening shadows hid his embarrassment.

"Hope I didn't interrupt anything," Alva said.

"No—"

"Of course not—"

Dane and Lacy spoke at once, both their tones sounding suspiciously like that of children being caught red-handed with their fingers in an off-limits cookie jar.

Taking the offensive was what was needed here, Dane decided. Whipping up plenty of accusation, he asked, "Where have *you* been? Lacy's been waiting for hours."

Alva shrugged, and even in the dim, purplish light, Dane saw the man grimace.

"I got held up," he said. "I did get the battery, though." He turned his attention to Lacy. "Mind if I take care of putting it in in the morning? It'll be hard to see—"

"Sure," Lacy said. "I don't mind." Then she looked over at Dane. "As long as Dane doesn't mind putting me up one more night."

He saw the smile that hovered on her mouth. And he offered her one to match it.

His voice was whisper soft and raspy as hell as he told her, "I don't mind at all."

It was utterly amazing, Lacy thought, how one kiss could alter everything. She and Dane had had such fun after Alva left last night. There had been no more passionate encounters, but they had laughed and talked until late into the night.

The first time Dane expressed his embarrassment at nearly having been caught necking on the back porch, she'd grinned. The second time, she'd chuckled. Every time he bemoaned his humiliation after that, she'd laughed. By the time they'd said their good-nights, her stomach muscles were aching. The whole situation was quite comical.

They were both full-grown adults, she in her late thirties, Dane in his early forties. There should be no reason at all that they should feel uncomfortable over a simple kiss.

But that had been no simple kiss.

They had let the thing take control. No, that wasn't the full truth. They had invited it to come among them. They had reveled in its presence. Oh, how they had reveled.

Yes, their relationship had changed…and it was a change that had remained even after the sun rose. There was a playfulness now. A lighthearted teasing that had them both fairly floating as they had enjoyed their morning coffee before Dane had gone off to the barn.

"Hey," Dane called to her from the hallway now, "let's take a walk. There's something I want to show you."

My, but he was a good-looking man. She'd thought that when she'd first arrived. But now that the stress around his mouth had eased, and the tension in his gaze had cleared, he was devastatingly handsome. And Lacy was giddy with joy to think that the heated kiss they had shared in the glorious twilight had taken all the pressure off him. In fact, it had seemed to make him over into an entirely new man.

"But what about Alva?" she asked. "Now that the cattle are fed, he's started working on my car—"

"This will only take a few minutes," he said. "Then you can be on your way."

A shadow fell over the moment, and she felt her

forehead knit as a thought shrieked through her brain. Had it been the passionate encounter that had so improved his mood? Or was it the fact that she was leaving today that had him seeming so buoyant?

The doubt put a huge damper on her mood all of a sudden.

"Come." He held out his hand to her, his smoky-gray eyes soft and utterly fascinating.

Her uncertainty vanished, and she went to him, sliding her palm into his. When she'd approached him last night, meaning only to offer him comfort, she'd told him that she wanted nothing from him. And she had meant it. She was happy to live in the moment.

They left the house by the front door, and Dane shouted to Alva, "We won't be long."

The elderly man didn't even lift his head from under the hood, but only tossed them a wave before reaching for a wrench.

She and Dane walked across a vacant hilly meadow, and soon a small house came into view. It looked down-at-the-heels to say the least. The larger of the two front windows was spiderwebbed with long, jagged cracks. The one to the left of the door had no glass left in it at all. The front door was scarred, and it hung a bit cockeyed on its hinges. The clapboards were so weathered that the paint was worn down to bare wood in places. Lots of places.

"What is this place?" she finally asked, unable to curb her curiosity any longer.

"It was my dad's house. My house. It's where I grew up."

"You're kidding?" She knew the surprise in her tone probably sounded rude, but her query was out before she'd had time to restrain it. "I mean, it's so small. It must have only one bedroom."

"That's right," he told her. "And that's where Dad slept. I slept on the living-room sofa. I didn't have a room of my own until I married Helen, and Alva and I built the brick rancher I live in now."

She shook her head as she walked closer, peering through the cracked windowpane. "But I don't understand. Your father was half owner of the spread. Why were you and he living in such—"

Squalor was the word that came to mind. But instead, what she finished with was "—a small place?"

"Every time I asked him, he said this house was good enough for his parents, so it was good enough for us."

The little house was dismal. And Lacy could only imagine that living here would be a dreary existence. No wonder Dane had wanted to escape to college, to see and experience a little of the world before returning to work the spread.

"So your dad grew up here." It wasn't a question. "How about Alva? How did he come to have a partnership with your father?"

"My grandfather and Alva's father owned the place at one time. When Pap died—that's how Alva always referred to his dad—Alva inherited. As did my father when my grandfather died. All that happened before I was born."

So the land had been passed from father to son...yet, Dane's father had been about to break that tradition by disowning his only child just because he was following his dream. What kind of man had Bud Buchanan been? A tyrant, Lacy decided then and there, although she'd never say that aloud to Dane.

"So, why are we here?" she asked.

He stared at the ground for a moment, one hand on his hip, the other combing through his coal-black hair. He was a sturdy man. Well-built. Brawny, even. And knowing she'd be leaving here soon, Lacy allowed herself to feast on the sight of him.

His gaze was serious when he finally fastened onto her face.

"After everything I told you last night," he began, "I didn't want you getting the wrong impression about things. About my life."

Her forehead puckered when she heard the curious remark, but she remained quiet.

"I told you all those things so you'd understand why I can't risk being connected to anyone. Why I need to be on my own. Completely and totally."

The lone wolf. As he stood there, his gray eyes hooded, this analogy floated easily into Lacy's head.

"But I don't want you feeling bad for me," he continued. "I'm not unhappy. I'm not lonely. I'm fine. In fact, I'm very content. I have hard work to keep me busy. I have a thriving business. A nice home. A good friend in Alva." His head jerked to indicate the house in front of them. "See, I know what bad is. I know what misery is. I've come from it. Compared to that, my life now is good. It's very good." The summer air grew suddenly stiff as he shrugged and added, "I just wanted you to know that."

She searched his face a moment. Then she nodded. "Okay."

What she wanted to say was, *I hear what you're saying, but I don't believe a word that's coming out of your mouth.*

Oh, she didn't doubt that his childhood had been hard. But what she had no faith in whatsoever were his proclamations that he wasn't lonely, that his life was good just the way it was. What surprised her was that she didn't just blurt out the thought. Usually, she'd just speak her mind and have done with it. And why she didn't was beyond her.

No, it wasn't, she decided. The reason she'd kept the thought to herself was because Dane mattered. She cared about him. And telling him he was lying to her—lying to himself—would have been hurtful. And she just couldn't bring herself to hurt him.

She noticed then that Dane's attention was no longer focused on her, but on something near the door of the house. When she looked closer, she saw that it was broken glass. A broken beer bottle.

"Wait right here a second," he murmured, already starting for the door.

He disappeared inside.

The sun grew hot, the heat of the day had Lacy swiping her fingers across her brow. Without giving the action any thought at all, she started for the door of the dilapidated house.

"Be careful!"

His stern warning made her pause just inside the threshold.

"There's glass everywhere."

Lacy looked around. Bottles and aluminum cans were scattered here and there, on tabletops, on the floor. As he'd warned, broken glass was everywhere, as were smashed cans.

"Looks like Randy Wilson's been partying here."

"Now, how fair is that?" she said, feeling the need

to defend Dane's young neighbor. "You don't know it was Randy."

"I don't?" He pointed. "That's his helmet. The one I keep telling him to wear when he's riding, hell-bent, on that ATV of his. Guess he hasn't been wearing it lately because he left it behind here."

Lacy said no more. The evidence was pretty clear.

He started gathering up bottles and trash. "Listen," he told her, not looking in her direction, "I'm sure Alva's got your car ready. You should go on back. Get on your way. I'm going to stay here and clean up a bit."

The idea that this was where they'd make their goodbyes startled Lacy. "But don't you want to walk back with me? Don't you want to see me off?"

His shoulders rounded, his gaze swinging around to meet hers. He shook his dark head. "I don't think so." His voice was low. "There's plenty to do here."

For some reason, she couldn't let it go so easily. "B-but...can I call you? Once I get back to Richmond? It'd be great..."

She let the sentence trail when his head moved from side to side.

"That's not wise. I've already explained everything, Lacy. You know how I feel."

Yes, she did know. He didn't want to get close to anyone because he didn't want to disappoint them, fail them. But she'd told him she wouldn't ask anything from him. However, had she really meant that? She'd realized last night that her heart belonged to this man. That she'd spent her whole life loving him. Yet he was determined to keep a cool distance from her.

In an instant, she decided he was right. Severing the cord cleanly was the wisest thing to do.

"If that's the way you want it," she said. She turned toward the door. "Have a good life, Dane."

And she left.

As she walked back to Dane's house, she kept pushing aside the emotions that wanted to well in her. She didn't want to feel. If she had let herself, there would be sadness and disappointment, rejection and regret. But there would also be a sweet poignancy. She'd had a chance to see Dane again. To have rekindled in her the intense fire he'd sparked all those years ago. Even though he refused the friendship she offered, even though he'd refused to help her become pregnant, she was still happy she came. Happy she saw him again.

But all the emotions threatening her could come crashing in later, she thought as she put her car into gear. She needed to get home now. Needed to get back to her business. Back to her life. And with a backward wave at Alva, she headed down the driveway.

She turned onto the gravel road that would take her to the tiny bridge and to the main highway just beyond. But when she accelerated, a horrible noise erupted, the engine died and the car rolled to a stop. Lacy just shook her head in disbelief, got out of the car and lifted the hood. She saw the shredded remains of some kind of belt down among the engine parts.

Just then, Alva reached the car, huffing and puffing, evidently rushing to her rescue when he'd seen her car stall.

"Well, would you look at that." He reached down

and pulled the remnants of the black rubber from the engine. His milky eyes squinted against the sunshine. ''This timing belt is shot, missy. Looks like you won't be goin' anywhere.''

It seemed that going back to Richmond just wasn't written in the stars for her. She could stamp her foot and shout in frustration. She could kick the front bumper and slam her hand down on the fender. But she didn't do any of those things. Instead…

She laughed.

Chapter Nine

It took the automobile store two tries and two days to order in the proper timing belt for her car. If Lacy had known this up front, she'd have had Sharon come pick her up and then she'd have returned to Oak Flat during the weekend to pick up her car. As it was, she was missing nearly a full week of work, but it really couldn't be helped.

The first belt Alva had brought home on Wednesday hadn't fit, so he'd had to travel back to the automotive store only to come home around suppertime with the news that they didn't stock belts for sports cars. So the part was ordered and it did arrive within the promised twenty-four hours.

However, late Thursday afternoon, Alva told her the belt was the wrong size for her car, and another was on order, so she'd stayed yet another night.

Here it was Friday morning, and Lacy considered having Sharon come get her, but Alva convinced her that the car would soon be repaired.

"Do you think I ought to have the car towed to a mechanic?" she asked Dane.

He'd seemed so very reserved since he'd returned from his childhood home and found her sitting on his front porch. If she didn't know better, she'd say he'd actually acted suspicious. Although, she had no idea why he should feel wary. He'd explained that he wasn't interested in a relationship with her. That he wasn't even interested in a friendship. She just had to live with that.

Oh, he was quite sociable, but the playful teasing they had shared the night of and the morning after their kiss was gone. There had been times during the past two days when she'd caught him looking at her, and she'd felt that massive attraction swooping down on them. But each time, he'd glance away and go on with whatever chore he was doing.

"If you even suggested seeing a mechanic," Dane said, his eyes glinting merrily at the thought, "Alva would pitch a fit. His motto is, don't pay anyone to do what you can do for yourself."

Lacy glanced out the window and smiled. "Well, it looks like he's got himself some help."

Dane came up behind her, and unwittingly her eyes closed as she inhaled the scent of him. Oh, how she would miss him once she did return to Richmond.

"Randy."

He practically growled the boy's name and he set off for the front door.

"Now, Dane, don't go running him off. Alva might be making friends with him."

From where she stood at the window, she could see the teen's spine stiffen, his shoulders square defensively the instant Dane stepped out onto the porch and called his name.

"You've been drinking up at the old house."

It was not a question, but a blatant accusation.

"Have not."

But Lacy heard little conviction in Randy's tone.

"Where'd you get the beer?" Dane asked. "Don't you know you could get into a lot of trouble, drinking at your age? That's private property you're destroying out there."

Lacy's heart went out to the boy when she heard the barrage of reprimanding questions. There was such sternness lacing Dane's tone, she'd have been terribly distressed if she'd had to face him. Randy remained silent, his face growing red and he started to turn away. But Alva's hand on his shoulder stopped him.

"Hold on, son," Alva said. "Let's straighten this out. It's gonna be all right." The older man directed his gaze at Dane. "Now, why would Randy do such a thing? He's a smart boy. He wouldn't be drinking. How do you know it's not some of the other kids from town going to the old house to party?"

"I've got proof."

Lacy left the window then. She picked up the helmet that sat on the coffee table. If Randy fled, she wanted to give him the chance to take it with him. He'd need it the next time he went riding.

She stepped out onto the porch and stood just behind, but to one side of, Dane. As soon as Alva and Randy saw her with the helmet, a couple different things happened. The elderly man's eyes widened just a fraction, then his face registered disappointment when he glanced over at the teenager. The only sign of emotion on Randy's face was an almost imperceptible frown. Lacy couldn't tell if he was feeling ashamed, or if he was merely irritated by having gotten caught.

"There are broken beer bottles all over out there," Dane said.

Randy's jaw tensed and his chin tipped up in defiance. "Sometimes I get angry."

"Well, I suggest you find some other way to express your feelings." After a moment, Dane added, "Stay away from the old house."

He turned on his heel, nearly colliding with her. She clearly conveyed her feelings about his behavior by giving him a good glare. Oh, the child had needed a good talking-to, that wasn't what upset her. But the manner in which Dane had handled the matter was what made her fume. Shouting at Randy and then demanding that he keep off the property wasn't how things should have been done. It was so clear that the teen needed some positive attention. And it frustrated her that Dane refused to give it to him.

Dane met her gaze for a moment as if deciphering her thoughts, sidestepped her and entered the house.

Lacy offered the teenager a warm smile, then went down the porch steps and handed him the helmet.

"You wear this, now," she told him gently. "It would be a terrible thing if you got hurt."

His gaze averted and his mouth pursed sullenly. "Some people wouldn't think so."

Empathy stung her. "Oh, Randy," she said, reaching out and touching his forearm, "that's not true."

Because he hadn't been specific, she couldn't say who he accused of not caring about his welfare; his parents, Dane, or simply the world at large. She remembered being a teen. Remembered how she'd felt. Awkward, unloved and lonely. Sudden anger roiled inside her. But she hid her feelings behind a smile.

"You helping to fix my car?" she asked him.

Randy shrugged, then turned to Alva. Lacy knew the teen was checking to see if he was still welcome.

"He sure is," Alva said. "And I could use some help, too. This job is bigger than I'd first imagined."

"Then—" Lacy backed away "—I'll let the two of you get to it."

She marched into the house and made a beeline for Dane.

"How could you treat that poor boy like that?"

"Treat him like what?" was his response. "I offered him some friendly advice. He shouldn't be drinking. And he shouldn't be trespassing on private property."

"Friendly advice my foot," she grumbled. "Why can't you be pleasant to the boy? Would it kill you to offer him a little of your time? Can't you see he's lonely? That he's hurting?"

"Look, Lacy," Dane said, his gray gaze narrowing, "Randy Wilson is none of my concern. He's got parents. Let them look after him." In frustration, he rubbed his hand over his mouth. "The only thing my father gave me that was any good was a life philosophy. Work hard and keep your life unencumbered. That's my plan. I get up every day and tend to my business. *My* business. Not anyone else's. That's what's best for everybody."

"You can't seriously believe that. You really want to fashion your life after Bud Buchanan?"

"Don't speak ill of my father," Dane said. "You didn't know the man."

"Maybe I didn't. But I've learned enough about him this past week to know he was a...a..."

Fear suddenly shot through her and she went quiet. She hadn't meant to start an argument. She hadn't meant to become judge and jury on his father's personality. She'd only meant to take up for young Randy, who didn't seem to have anyone to take up for him.

She forced her ire aside and the tension in her shoulders released. "I don't want to fight. I just think you and Alva could help that boy."

"Alva can do what he wants," Dane said. "But I've got work to do."

And he walked out of the room. She heard the door close as he left the house.

Lacy sighed. She knew exactly why Dane didn't want to befriend Randy. The man was afraid he couldn't live up to whatever it was the teenager was needing. Whatever it was he was looking for. It was sad. Dane had so much to offer. And he'd receive so much in return if he did reach out. His life would be enriched. His mind would be stimulated. And his heart...well, his heart just might come alive again. She couldn't help but wonder what she could say or do to make him understand all these things.

"Alva and Randy are still working on my car," she said to Dane as she stepped out onto the back porch late that same evening. "So you might have to suffer through having me spend another night."

He motioned for her to join him. "You've been no trouble, Lacy. Honest." He sighed. "I know I haven't been a very good host."

The memory of the kiss they'd shared in this very

place came to her mind and she smiled. "Oh, I'd say you've done okay."

He studied her face for a moment, and a light glinted in his smoky eyes, telling her he realized what was on her mind. He smiled.

Ever since their irritated exchange that afternoon, Lacy had contemplated how she might go about talking to Dane about his "plan" to remain free and unfettered where caring for others was concerned.

Oh, he didn't see his plan in that light, she knew. He saw this disconnection he was forcing on himself as the only means of not failing those around him.

But either way, he was losing out. And she wanted to tell him that.

She also realized how very much she missed that playful teasing they had shared just days ago. And she'd come to the conclusion that if she could somehow rekindle the lighthearted banter, the mischievous teasing, then expressing herself about his plan would be easier.

Now that they were both on the same wavelength, so to speak, by remembering the kiss they had shared, she thought now was the perfect time to take things to a higher level.

A spontaneous, utterly naughty query popped into her mind.

"Tell me, Dane," she began, tossing him a impish grin, "what does a man like you…a man who's determined to avoid intimate interaction…a man who's settled on remaining single…what does a man like that do for sex?"

She chuckled at the surprise she read in his gaze. "I mean, I do understand that sex and love aren't the same thing. But you're a healthy male. And all humans need a little…um, comfort now and then.'' The special inflection she placed on the word comfort would give him no choice but to realize exactly what she meant.

Controlling his initial surprise sure didn't take him long. His eyes leveled on her. ''Nervy comments like that just might scare off a man who happened to be the least bit reserved. Why do you feel the need to shock people like that? Intimidate them? You trying to keep men at arm's length? Is that what happened to your marriage, Lacy? Did you scare your husband off?''

The gasp she expelled was sharp, his softly spoken questions striking her to the core. She was stunned speechless and didn't know how to respond.

He looked immediately contrite. ''I'm sorry,'' he murmured. ''I was only thinking of giving you a taste of your own medicine. I crossed the line. I truly am sorry.''

She sat there thinking about what he'd said, what he'd asked…what he was implying. And she had to admit that all her life she'd done just that. Blurted out her outrageous opinions with little to no thought of the feelings of others.

Why? she wondered. Was she somehow lashing out at men in general due to the rejection she'd experienced? From her father. From Dane. *Was* her intent to keep men at bay? Had the rejection she'd experienced done something to mess up her self-esteem? Skew her thinking about her self-worth?

But she was successful. She was independent. Intelligent. *Thriving*.

It didn't make sense. If she was thriving, then why was she so plagued with this urgent need to have a child? Why was she so desperate for someone to love?

The questions closed in on her, threatening to suffocate her. But she shoved her way out of the choking fog. She couldn't deal with it now. She just couldn't face all those daunting issues at this moment.

"It's okay," she forced herself to say. The smile she offered him felt plastic. "Tit for tat. You're absolutely correct. I had no right asking you such a personal question."

They sat listening to the quiet for a moment.

Finally, Dane said, "Actually, if you don't mind telling me, I really would like to hear what happened between you and your husband. How long were you married? And how come the relationship didn't work out?"

Lacy sighed and relaxed against the chair back. "It was my fault." This time her sad smile was genuinely felt. "It really was. I feel so bad about the whole thing. Richard really did want our marriage to work. And I tried." A second sigh issued forth. "But I guess we never really should have married in the first place."

She studied the trees and meadow, barely registering how beautifully the scene glowed in the moonlight. "You see," she continued, "Richard and I met at work, not long after I'd graduated. I was working for a computer firm that offered technical services to area businesses on a contract basis. I learned so much there. Richard and I quickly worked our way up to manager level. He seemed to fall head over heels in love with me. I wasn't really sure how I felt about him. The attention was nice and all. But…"

Her thoughts trailed. It wouldn't be nice to express

all her disappointments in her ex-husband. The lack of stimulating conversation. His disinterest in current events. His apathy toward anything and everything, really, that didn't involve computers. Not to mention his—there was no delicate way to put this—lack of proficiency in the lovemaking department. There was no romance. No petting. No touching. No "necking," as Dane had called it.

Recalling the passionate exchange between herself and Dane, she couldn't help but smile.

Just then Alva rounded the corner, his form nothing more than a dark shadow, and called out, "Car's ready. But I sure hope you're not planning on leaving tonight. It's too late. I'm going to drive Randy home so the boy doesn't have to walk in the dark."

"Thanks for letting us know, Alva," Dane told him.

"Yes, Alva," Lacy said, but the elderly man had already turned and disappeared from sight. She scooted to the end of the chair. "Guess I should be on my way."

He reached out and took her hand. Lights flashed. Energy sparked. And Lacy felt the need to suck in air through her rounded lips. But she restrained the reaction.

"Alva's right," Dane said. "Wait until morning." He pulled his hand away from her. "Go on with your story," he urged quietly.

She shrugged. "The only thing I can say is that Richard and I didn't have a whole lot in common. But somehow I let him talk me into marriage. Like I said, I really tried. So did Richard. But we were just wrong for each other. Once we broke up, I left the company, took back my maiden name and started my own business. And I've been fine ever since.''

She did blame herself for the failing of her marriage, although she'd been wrong all this time about why her marriage had failed. She'd thought it was her unfair comparison. Richard never really measured up to her memories of Dane.

Now, after spending time with Dane, after experiencing the joy of being in his arms, kissing his lips, she knew why her marriage had failed. It wasn't that Richard hadn't measured up…it was that she'd been in love with Dane the whole time, and she simply hadn't known it. She couldn't ever be happy with another man. And even though she knew she and Dane would never be a couple, the realization of her feelings—of the true reason behind her breakup with Richard—was liberating.

The night was quiet, and Lacy stared out into the darkness, listening to the mournful lowing of the cattle, thinking about all the things she'd said about her marriage…all the things she'd learned about herself. The feel of Dane's hand sliding over top hers startled her. Her gaze swung around to meet his.

''Thanks for telling me.''

His tone was as soft as the southern night. It seemed to hug Lacy, wrapping her in a protective embrace.

''I'd been driving myself crazy wondering how a man could bring himself to let you go…once he'd captured you.''

The tenderness in the statement, the romance of his words, made her feel like a starry-eyed schoolgirl.

Lord, how easily this man could steal away her breath, rob her brain of all thought. Once again, the question resonated through her mind, how would she ever live without him?

Chapter Ten

Early the following morning, Lacy and Dane were having their morning coffee together. By the time she awoke, Dane was usually out in the barn doing some chore, feeding the cattle, herding them from one grassy pasture to another. So having him here with her was a real treat.

"It's so beautiful here," she told him. "So quiet. And relaxing."

"Surely you miss all that city excitement."

His gray eyes glittered teasingly, and Lacy smiled.

The air between them was once again cozy. After having made that tender comment last night, he seemed less tense around her. He certainly was as changeable as the wind, it seemed. On his guard one moment, teasing her the next. But she knew he was dealing with a lot. The baggage from his past was heavy.

"Actually, I haven't missed Richmond a bit," she

admitted. "Who needs to go to museums to see gorgeous landscape paintings when you can look out the back door and see the real thing? And who needs the supermarket when you can buy fresh, homegrown veggies from your neighbors? Who needs the traffic? Who needs all the people? Who needs—"

His laughter cut her off. "I'm glad to hear you appreciate country living. But what about your job? What about your business?"

She shrugged. "I could do my job from anywhere." She'd never in a million years admit that she'd lain awake nights pondering how wonderful it would be to promote her assistant, Sharon, to office manager in order to free herself to work from home. Dane's home.

"As long as I have access to the Internet," she said, "and a decent computer system, I can earn a living." The coffee tasted good when she took a swallow. "It's true that I'd have to travel a little, to meet with clients and such, but I don't have to do that very often. I hate to brag—" she grinned "—but my reputation in the Web world is pretty good. Clients come looking for me most of the time these days."

The information seemed to please him to no end, and Lacy felt warm all over to think that he just might be proud of her accomplishments. Then she felt discomfited over having boasted, and before she realized it she was battling a sudden case of timidity.

The mere notion of her feeling shy was pretty funny to her and she chuckled.

"What?" he asked.

"Nothing." She shook her head, unwilling to reveal the thought behind her humor. It was amazing to her that, during the past week, this man had made her run the gamut of emotions; she'd felt amorous and needy, raucous and fun-loving, confident, poised, uncertain, reserved, wary, apprehensive and downright nervous. It was almost as if she were once again plopped back into those volatile adolescent years.

But then, a quiet thought echoed across her mind: maybe true love is forever young, full of whimsy, hope and excitement.

Dane was her true love. Tiny chills coursed across her skin. She'd wondered for years why she'd never found the man of her dreams. Now she discovered that she had found him. Years ago. But fate—and circumstances—had kept them apart.

A deep sadness covered her like a cloak as she realized that they'd never have a chance to be together. Dane just couldn't seem to break the bonds of his past.

Unwilling to wallow in misery during her last few moments with him, Lacy forced herself to brighten. "So how come you're still here this morning? You're usually hard at work at this hour."

His slate gaze averted. "Oh, I don't know…just needed a few extra minutes to wake up this morning, I guess."

She burst out laughing. "That's the lamest lie I've ever heard told."

He had sense enough not to push his story further. "Okay, okay, let's just say I wanted to see you off…*safely* this time. That poor car of yours can't take much more abuse."

What an odd thing for him to say. She frowned. "What do you mean?" And before he had time to answer, the inference in his statement struck her. "What are you saying? That my car is being damaged…"

Her mouth actually dropped open when she finally understood his full meaning. "You think I'm sabotaging my car." Irritation flared. "Now, why on earth would I do that?"

He chuckled at her indignant reaction, and that only caused her ire to blaze hotter.

"Come on now, admit it," he said, grinning like the Cheshire cat himself. "You wanted to hang around, hoping that you'd be able to use that persuasive tongue of yours to talk me into 'donating' to your cause."

Indignation pumped through her veins, flushing her face and loosening her hold on the thoughts bursting to life in her head.

"Why, you big oaf," she said. "How dare you make fun of me? I'd never jeer at someone else's hopes and dreams."

"Wait a minute—"

"Why," she rushed on, "how would it make you feel if I were to make a joke of some of the things going on in your life? Like that plan of yours to remain all alone…I mean, how stupid is that?"

Rather than wound him, rather than shock that grin off his face, as she'd planned, her diatribe only made him beam. Seems the only thing she'd smacked with her remarks was his funny bone.

"Okay," he said, throwing up his hands, palms out. "I shouldn't have made light of your dreams…and I do apologize. From the bottom of my heart. But you've got to admit it, Lacy. The jig is up. You've been tinkering with your car.''

Her gaze narrowed and she lifted her hand, holding her thumb and index finger a half inch apart. ''If I was this much less dignified, I'd tell you exactly what you could do with your jig, Dane Buchanan.'' She set down her mug with such force that coffee sloshed over the rim and onto the table.

''Aw, now look what you've done.'' Humor rippled around edges of his tone. ''You've made a mess.''

''You'll have plenty of time on your hands to clean it up once I leave.'' She stood and then stomped out of the kitchen and into the living room where her purse and packed bag sat waiting.

''Hold on a minute,'' he called, trailing after her. ''Don't go away angry.''

''I get your message loud and clear. Don't go away angry. Just go away. Well, I'm leaving. Right now.''

She was out the door and down the porch steps before he caught her. His hand on her shoulder made her whip around to face him. ''I'm not going to stay here a minute longer.''

''Don't leave like this.'' His voice was quiet, suddenly disconcerted. ''I sure didn't mean to make you angry.''

Lacy turned to slip the key into the truck's lock…and it was then that both of them realized that the hood of her car was raised.

''I thought Alva said the belt was fixed. That the car was ready to go,'' she said.

''So did I.''

Automatically, they moved along the side of the

car. Lacy's eyes widened in surprise when she saw Dane's father-in-law standing there, a screwdriver in one hand and some car part in the other.

"Alva, what are you doing?" Dane asked. "What's wrong with Lacy's distributor cap? I thought—"

"Well, it's cracked now," Alva said, annoyance thick in his tone. "It would have been just fine if the two of you hadn't scared the dickens out of me runnin' out of the house like that. I'd only planned to take it off and loosen some of the wires, but that door burst open and you barged out of the house. I tried to get it back on too quick. I tightened down on the screw too hard and cracked the dad-blamed thing. Now we're going to have to buy a brand-new one."

"So it was you." Dane planted his hands on his hips. "I've just made a fool of myself by blaming Lacy for tearing up her car, and all this time it's been you." His dark head shook back and forth. "I should have known."

"Yes, it's been me. And don't hold your breath waiting for an apology 'cause you're bound to faint dead away before you hear one." The elderly man waved the tool and the distributor cap in his agitation. "Ever since Lacy came around, you've been like a different man. I've never seen you so smilin' and lively. You've been downright perky, I don't mind sayin'. So how can you blame me for wantin' to keep her around a bit?"

"I've never been perky a day in my life," Dane grumbled, clearly insulted.

"The hell you haven't," Alva retorted. His feigned

anger was gone, but the sincerity in his words, in his eyes, couldn't be missed.

Lacy wanted to laugh in Dane's face. She felt terribly vindicated. She wanted so badly to poke him in the chest and say, see, I told you so. How could she possibly sabotage her car, anyway, when she didn't know a timing belt from a distributor cap? But looking into his face and seeing his expression, she didn't dare speak her thoughts.

Storm clouds gathered in his eyes. "I do hope, Alva, that you're planning on buying a new distributor cap today and getting this car in driving condition."

"Of course I was. Right after I do my chores—"

"I'll do your chores," Dane said. "You get on the road." He left them, then, stomping off to the barn.

The air was tight from all those harsh words that had been flung around, and it was clear to her that Alva was worried about her being angry. Lacy felt the need to lighten things up and let him know she didn't harbor any ill feelings.

"Wow," she said to him. "He sure seems steamed." The grin that hovered around her mouth, along with the playful inflection she'd placed in the opinion, made it clear to him that she wasn't the least upset by his actions.

The elderly man looked relieved. Finally, he chuckled. "Oh, he'll get over it. He always gets over my antics pretty quick."

"So you do this kind of thing often."

His smile widened. Indicating the distributor cap he held in his hand with a flicking gaze, he said, "Well, now, not *this* kind of thing."

They both laughed.

"I don't usually go to these lengths," he continued. "I do have to admit, though, I've been trying to fix up Dane for a while now. He just hasn't been interested."

Tell me about it, Lacy nearly mumbled. But she kept quiet.

"You see—" bending over, he chucked his screwdriver into the toolbox that sat by his feet and then straightened, catching Lacy's eye "—I owe that boy. I owe him more than I'll ever be able to repay."

For a moment, Alva went quiet as he let his gaze wander over to Dane's retreating figure. Once his son-in-law disappeared into the barn, Alva swiveled his gaze back to Lacy's face.

"My Helen was—" the man paused long enough to swallow "—special."

Lacy nodded. "Dane told me about her…condition."

"Her mama died when she was born," he said. "So Helen was all I had. For a lotta years. She was so shy. So insecure. She fought going to school, tooth and nail. I barely got the child to finish high school," he said. "She was so…what's that word…reclusive. She was terribly conscious of how she looked. How she walked. She had no friends besides Dane. And she loved that boy with all her heart and soul. She did what she could for Dane when Bud was alive. I did, too. We both knew that getting Dane to college was important."

Alva reached up and scratched his scalp through his thick, granite-gray hair.

"I was shocked when he asked Helen to marry

him," he continued. "He didn't love my daughter. Not—" color tinged his cheeks "—passionately. Like a man should love his wife. He was beholden to her, that was all. And I should have stopped the wedding. I really should have done right by Dane by making him see he shouldn't sacrifice his own happiness for my little girl's. But, you see, she was my only child. And I could see how planning for the wedding was making her so happy."

He gazed off, remembering. "So happy, I thought my heart was gonna melt away just watching her face beam like pure, radiant sunshine." He sighed then, his cloudy eyes finding Lacy's again. "They didn't have a bad relationship. She was totally dedicated to Dane, and he really cared about her. Was gentle with her. And that child they made together—" now his eyes misted with tears "—was a blessing sent straight from heaven."

Sniffing, Alva swiped gruffly at his eyes. "Dane fulfilled Helen's dreams. He made her a wife. And a mother. And that was something she thought she'd never have. Now that my little girl and her Angel are gone, Dane's all I've got left. I'd move heaven and earth to see him happy. He deserves some joy after all he's sacrificed for me and mine."

They didn't have a bad relationship. He didn't love my daughter. Not passionately.

Alva's words ran through her head. When Dane had talked about Helen, Lacy had noticed that he hadn't used the word *love* when describing his feelings for the woman. Bringing Helen's dreams to fruition by marrying her, giving her a child, had been a selfless act on Dane's part. He must have felt terribly grateful to her for caring for his father while he was away. That college education he wanted so badly seemed to have cost him a great deal. But then his daughter came to mind, and Lacy thought of the years Dane had enjoyed loving his little girl, and she knew he hadn't come away totally empty-handed. She'd bet her last dollar that Dane wouldn't have given up his daddy experience for all the gold in the world.

However, for the life of her, she couldn't understand why Bud Buchanan had been so unreasonable about his son's wanting to go away to school. Maybe the man thought Dane would get a taste of life away from the spread and decide not to return. Maybe he was afraid of being alone. Maybe he'd been ill for a long time before Dane actually discovered that fact, and the man simply felt he needed someone. She thought of questioning Dane's father-in-law about Bud, but felt it really wasn't any of her business.

"I'm sorry about messin' with your car," Alva said sheepishly. "But I couldn't think of any other way to keep you here." He chuckled. "That weather we had last week helped me out. Remember tellin' me that we should send energy to the storm system…hoping it would move out of the area?"

Lacy nodded at the memory.

"I hope you don't mind, but I prayed fervently for those clouds to hang around."

They laughed together.

"It's okay," she told him. "I understand."

Alva's expression turned serious. "There's something special between you and Dane. I saw it early on. And I've never seen Dane so lively. So energetic. Having you here has been good for him."

Stepping toward the elderly man, she planted an affectionate kiss on his cheek. His eyes went wide with surprise, and he flushed to his hairline and Lacy had to chuckle at him.

"What was that for?" he asked.

"For caring about Dane." Reaching out, she swiped her finger through the dust coating her car fender. "I think Dane and I have something special, too, Alva. But we've got a problem. He isn't going to let me into his heart. I've tried to talk to him about what we feel for each other. And these feelings have actually swept us away a couple of times. I—I know he recognizes that there's something between us, but…"

"He's just too gol-durned stubborn—"

"No." She shook her head. "I'm not sure stubbornness has anything to do with it. I think he's afraid. I'm sure he is. He won't let anyone in…he won't care about anyone…me, or young Randy, or anyone, because he's afraid he'll fail us."

"Like he failed Helen and Angel." Sadness misted Alva's eyes. "He feels responsible for the accident, I know."

"He feels he failed his father, too."

The old man's mouth pursed tightly at the mention of Bud Buchanan and he shook his head. But he didn't say anything more for a moment. Then he said, "I've thought for a long time that Dane's fallen into a deep dark hole and he won't reach out for the willing hands of those who want to pull him out." He lifted one shoulder. "I've come to the conclusion that this is a hole he's just going to have to climb out of himself."

The Dane she knew twenty years ago would have been strong enough to pull himself out of this, Lacy thought. He could answer any question, solve any problem, face any crisis. But she wondered, with the passing of all these years, if he'd become comfortable in his misery. Sometimes it took less energy to continue traveling in the same well-worn furrows than it was to break free and make a change.

"You might not think stubbornness has anything to do with this," Alva finally said. "But I tend to think it does. See, I knew that boy's daddy. And there wasn't a more stubborn man in all the world. So Dane came by it honest. Pigheadedness is in his blood."

Chapter Eleven

At noon, Lacy went looking for Dane. She found him checking over the calves that had been born earlier in the spring. He looked in their ears, examined their eyes, checked every inch of their sturdy bodies. The babies were so ugly that they were cute as could be. And the plaintive little mewing sounds they made were endearing.

Stepping up on the first rail of the wooden fence, she rested her elbows on the top one. Dane's biceps bulged as he subdued one of the animals in front of him, yet his touch was lamb gentle. Watching him work was thrilling for her. Something she knew she'd never tire of.

"Hey, there," she said.

He didn't look up from the calf he was inspecting. "I guess I owe you a big apology."

"Yeah, I guess you do."

Evidently, he couldn't figure out what to make of

the long-suffering in her remark. When he looked at her, there was quandary in his eyes. She chuckled at him.

"Oh, would you get over it, Dane? Okay, so I was a little angry at being accused of sabotage. But that's water under the bridge."

"A little angry?"

"Okay," she relented, "a lot angry. I was livid, actually. But the moment is gone. So are all the bad feelings. Let's move on. Life is too short to dwell on such things."

"That's easier for some people than it is others," he murmured.

The loaded statement was just waiting to open up some dialogue, and Lacy would have tackled it for all she was worth if she thought anything she'd have said would change his way of thinking.

Guess he's got to crawl out of that hole himself, Alva had said.

"Anything I can do to help?" she asked.

"Yes," he said. "There're only two calves left waiting to be looked at. Why don't you bring me one?"

"Aye, aye, Captain." Climbing down from her perch, she opened the gate just wide enough for her to squeeze though and then latched it securely behind her. "Any one in particular?"

"Either one."

For several minutes she attempted to capture the calves. She sashayed from side to side, until she got one cornered, but the quick little nipper slipped by her just as she was about to lay hands on it. Then she did the same to the other, blocking it in, arms flung wide, but just as she was about to get a secure hold on it, the darn thing nudged her—hard—and she fell on her butt with enough force that she could have sworn she saw whiffs of dust puff up from underneath her.

"Dane." She'd never whined before in her life, but frustration got the best of her. "What am I doing wrong?"

"Come here." He sounded as if he was losing patience with her. "You forgot this."

He took a length of rope that was hanging around one fence post.

"And what am I supposed to do with this?"

"Lasso 'em."

She just looked at him, not even bothering to reach for the rope.

"You don't know how to lasso? Wow, girl, you really are a city slicker." He shook his head dolefully.

"Yeah, well, the next time you're in front of your computer," she retorted, "try writing out some HTML codes. We all have our weaknesses."

He ignored her challenge. "I guess you could try this." Reaching into his pocket, he pulled out what must have been some kind of treat. He made a loud kissing sound and the calves came to him at a run.

"You ought to be ashamed." She glared at him, fists on hips. "You just apologized for picking on me this morning, and here you are again, acting like a big bully." She began slapping the dust from her rear.

His handsome face softened with a wonderful smile. "I know, Lacy. I don't know what's wrong with me. It's just that you're so darned pretty when you get all riled up."

That statement alone was almost enough for her to forgive him.

Almost.

She sidled up next to him and reached out to pet one of the calves between its ears. Placing her hip up snuggly next to Dane's, she gave him an abrupt and unceremonious nudge…right toward the water trough.

He scrambled to keep his balance, but in the end was forced to try to hop over the wooden trough. And his booted foot plopped right into the water. His jeans were soaked up to the knee. The shock on his face was highly entertaining.

"Why, you…"

He chased her. And she ran.

The calves scattered, mewing in confusion. The cows being housed in the adjacent pen began to call plaintively, clearly nervous about what was happening to their babies.

Dane caught her up in his arms and headed for the trough.

"You wouldn't dare." She tried valiantly to act incensed, but being in his arms was too exhilarating for her to express any real anger.

"Oh, wouldn't I?"

"Put me down."

"Whatever the lady wishes."

The next thing she knew, her rump made a splash and she was up to her chest in water. She scrambled out as quick as she could, and stood there sopping.

"I'm a mess."

Dane grinned. "Then we'd better go toss your shirt

and jeans into the washer. Not to mention those sneakers.''

Lacy looked down and saw that the white canvas of her sneakers was caked with dust and grime that was quickly turning to mud as water from her jeans ran in rivulets. She looked him in the face, saw the twinkle in his eye, and rather than feeling irritated or angry…

She felt full of lighthearted merriment, and she laughed.

She looked good in his T-shirt. Shadows of the dusky coins of her nipples barely showed through the soft cotton fabric. And his boxers sure never looked like that when he wore them. The hem struck her midthigh. She had nice legs. Miles of creamy skin and sculpted muscle. Her blond hair looked darker now that it was still damp from the shower she'd taken.

They sat in the coolness of the living room, the shades pulled against the noonday sun, as they waited for the dryer to finish its cycle. The silence was comfortable, and he felt very content. Dane liked the fact that Lacy didn't feel the need to fill every second with useless prattle.

This woman had a way of taking his emotions and turning them every which way but loose. He was often left feeling as if she stuffed them, and him, too, into an oak barrel and rolled the whole shooting match down a rocky mountainside. When he was near her, he was always feeling topsy-turvy. In a constant state of chaos.

And he'd never felt more alive.

Alva had been right in his assumption that Lacy's presence had changed the very air around here. Although Dane would never admit it out loud, he *had* felt rather perky. He nearly chuckled when his father-in-law's description of him came floating through his thoughts.

Dane had experienced about every emotion imaginable this past week because of Lacy. She made him feel like Rip van Winkle from childhood folklore; asleep for a hundred years until she'd arrived and tapped him on the shoulder…kissed him on the mouth. This revitalization he was experiencing had even weakened his resolve to stick to his well-honed plan of remaining alone. Waking up next to Lacy every day sure seemed like an awfully sweet way to spend the rest of his life. But every instinct in him told him to go back to sleep…that ignoring her and all the powerful feelings she stirred was the smart thing—the only thing—to do. Still, the thoughts lingered…

"Tell me about Angel."

Her request hit him like a sucker punch directly to the jaw.

"Do you mind my asking?"

"No," he said, his voice sounding like the croaking of a frog. "I don't mind." He swallowed, and his throat was so dry it was painful. Memories of his baby girl did that to him.

"She was the most beautiful creature on God's earth," he said. "I remember holding her for the first time. That soft baby smell. Those big, dark eyes taking in everything around her. The way she gripped my finger when I touched her tiny palm." Again, he swallowed. "She grew like a little weed. She called me Dad-a when she was finally able to talk. She added that extra short 'a' sound onto the ends of most words. We never knew why. We just thought it was cute. I loved listening to her talk."

He stared at the floor. "Once she hit about five, she was filled with questions. Chock-full of them. Why this, Dad-a? And why that, Dad-a? How come, Dad-a? I never got tired of her questions. Never. I wanted her to know everything." A rusty-sounding chuckle escaped him. "And she was bound and determined that I tell her everything, too."

The lump of emotion that rose in his throat made it hard to breathe. "It was bad, Lacy. The car wreck. A father isn't supposed to bury his little girl. That's not the way life is meant to work."

He gazed over at where Lacy sat on the other end of the sofa, quiet, absorbed in his discourse. Her azure eyes pained right along with him, and the urge to hug her to him welled up. Strongly. But he squelched it. For both their sakes.

"I thought I'd go insane with the grief."

Insane. That's exactly what he'd felt in the days, weeks and months directly following the crash that took his family from him. The darkness that swallowed him had been inky black. Even after all this time, it often threatened to fall in on him like a wobbling brick wall if he wasn't diligent in watching for it, shoring it up. Keeping the grief imprisoned.

"I know it might sound crazy..."

Her voice was silky soft on his ears, comforting, yet he sensed a reluctance in her, as if she was uncertain about what she was about to say.

"I know a person can't grieve for a baby that's never been born," she haltingly continued. "But in some strange way, that's exactly how I feel. Like I'm mourning the child I haven't even given birth to."

He watched as both her hands moved to cover her tummy. The action was so wholly innocent and unwitting that Dane felt the emotion that was already in his throat swell until he nearly had to struggle to inhale.

"So I do believe I can understand—at least a little—what you're suffering."

Oh, heaven help him. Hot emotion burned his eyelids, scalded his throat. He had known Lacy was desperate for a baby. She'd explained her despair. Her need. But now that she'd compared the anguish she endured to the monstrous grief he experienced himself, he felt he finally understood the true depth of the yearning that was pushing Lacy to become pregnant.

Reaching out, she placed the flat of her hand over his heart. Her skin felt warm, soothing through the thin cotton fabric of his shirt.

"I'm sorry you lost your child."

A single tear escaped the inner corner of her eye, trailing, as lonely and desolate as he often felt, down her cheek. Unable to watch its journey any longer, he gently swiped it away.

"And I'm sorry I can't help you have yours."

It was late that afternoon and Dane was replacing a length of rusty fencing with fresh barbed wire when Alva approached him. Being within sight of the house, Dane had observed his father-in-law and young Randy while the car repairs had been going on. He'd also watched Alva's advance, the head-dipping, hat-removing, telling Dane that his father-in-law was moving toward him with some caution.

"You still mad at me?" Alva asked when he got close.

"Nah," Dane replied. He offered up a smile of proof. He knew his father-in-law's matchmaking had been made with all good intentions.

"When it comes to matters of the heart," Alva said, "you know I usually mind my own business."

Remembering how Alva had tried to push the single women of Oak Flat in his path over the past months, this statement nearly made Dane snicker, but he was able to quell it before it escaped. Instead, he just dipped his head to hide his grin.

"But, Dane," the elderly man continued, "Lacy's leavin' today, so I feel I just gotta speak my mind."

Dane sighed. But he remained silent, respectfully lifting his gaze to look Alva in the eye.

"The two of you are meant to be together. That's clear as crystal to me. You've got to see it, too."

Clamping his top lip between his teeth, Dane once again pondered the wonderment that would be added to his life if Lacy were a constant part of it. It was wrong to think about the idea. But he thought about it, just the same.

"That spark I see between you is too danged strong to have popped up in the last week," Alva said. "I can't help but think it was there back when the two of you knew each other in college."

Dane's eyes went wide.

"I been thinking that, if it hadn't been for Helen, you and Lacy would have been together." Strong emotion choked the man, and he coughed. "You'd have been together all this time."

Guilt swam in Dane's head. "I was happy with Helen, Alva. I mean that."

"I know you were, boy. I know it." Alva placed his hand on Dane's shoulder and gave it a squeeze. "And Helen was happy. She sure was. But she's gone, and you've got some livin' left to do—"

"Lacy and I are from two different worlds." Dane turned back to his work. He didn't want to talk about this. It was dangerous. Contemplating a future that involved Lacy. Too dangerous.

Too many things could go wrong. Too many ways he could fail.

"You're thinking of your mama, aren't you, boy?"

He wasn't. But right now he'd grasp onto any reason, any motive, any memory—no matter how depressing—that would help him repress his desire to hold Lacy forever.

"You're thinking about how she left you. About how she and your dad were so different. About how this life was so hard for her that she up and left." Alva removed his hat, swiped his forearm across his brow. "Well, I don't care what Bud tried to make you believe, your ma didn't leave here because of you. She loved you with all her heart. And she didn't leave because life out here was hard. She left—" the old man's eyes narrowed, crinkling at the corners "—because your Daddy was a mean ol' cuss who insisted on controlling everyone around him. He tried to control me. And he tried his damnedest to control your every move. Yolanda was being smothered to death. She knew it. Hell, she wasn't allowed to leave the property by herself. So she decided that leavin' Bud for good was her only choice. And she knew your daddy would make her life a living hell—yours, too—if she took you with her. He'd have never given up on finding you. Bringing you back here. Never. He felt you belonged to him.''

That ever-present guilt swam around in Dane's head. Anger dived into the pool of his thoughts, as well. And bitterness. If all Alva was saying was true, he wondered, then why had his father given up on him in the end?

''Lacy's different from your mama,'' Alva continued.

Instantly, thoughts of Lacy calmed the turmoil roiling through Dane's mind. She had a way of doing that. She helped him, even when she wasn't physically present.

''She's stronger. And you sure aren't your daddy. You're a better man than him. A much better man.'' He nodded. ''You and Lacy. You should be together.''

You should be together. Alva's words reverberated in his head. Dane would love to think that was the truth. But why, he wondered, did doubt keep descending like a shroud?

''Besides, there's a real good reason why I'd like to see you attached and settled.''

The brightness in Alva's tone had Dane blinking, focusing on his father-in-law.

''I've got some living left to do, myself.'' Alva chuckled, his eyes glittering with a secret. ''I've met me a lady. You know her. It's Lottie's mother. Me and Belinda, we've been doing a little courting.'' His grin widened. ''She's really somethin'—''

Just then, the sound of an engine revving caught Dane's attention and he looked toward the house.

''What's Randy doing in Lacy's car?''

''Oh, I told him he could start the engine. Make sure it runs smooth.''

But the expressions on both men's faces quickly turned to horror when the back tires kicked up a slew of gravel and the car shot forward—crashing dead center into a fence post, shearing it off at ground level, and then pitching into a ditch.

Chapter Twelve

Dane paced the ER waiting room like a caged tiger. And each time he reached one end of the room, he'd turn and spew off another "well, if—" statement.

"Well, if we hadn't allowed the boy to come around," he'd said, "he wouldn't be in there getting stitches in his forehead."

"Well, if his parents hadn't been off in Richmond, they'd be here for the poor kid now."

"Well, if we'd have known he didn't know a gas pedal from a brake pedal, we would have stayed closer to him when he started that car."

Alva had been just as bad with his "who knew—" questions.

"Who knew the kid had never started a car before?"

"Who knew—"

"Stop!" Lacy said. "These what-ifs and who-knews aren't doing us any good. So just cut it out." She narrowed her eyes on Dane. "I can tell that you're really looking for some reason to feel guilty about all this. Well, don't. There was no way for you to foresee this happening. No way. So just focus on feeling relieved that Randy wasn't hurt any worse than he was.''

Dane sat down.

Lacy glanced at Alva. "I do hope," she said, "that this accident doesn't stop you from spending time with that young man—"

"Hell, Lacy," Dane cut in, "the crash is proof positive that the boy shouldn't be anywhere near our place."

"And why is that?" she asked, leveling her gaze onto him. "Because you'll fail him?"

Good, she thought. She'd shocked him. That's exactly the reaction she'd hoped for. Seeing him try to blame himself for something that was nothing more than an accident made her snap. She'd been nice to him…protected his feelings for far too long. It was high time he faced the truth.

"Just like you failed your dad?"

His expression grew taut and anger smoldered in his gray eyes. "That's exactly why. Listen, Lacy, why don't you just leave me be? Why don't you just go back to Richmond where you belong?"

The tone he used was hushed but ominous to the extreme. Anyone else would have backed down. But not Lacy.

"Oh, I plan to," she told him. "As soon as I can find a means of getting myself there. But I won't be leaving without speaking my mind first. And I want you to know, I don't believe you failed your father at all. In fact, I think he was the one who failed you."

His jaw tensed and relaxed, tensed and relaxed.

"I mean, what kind of father refuses to let his son reach for his dream? What kind of father tries to keep his son tied to his side? A tyrant, I say."

There. She'd said it. And if hearing her opinion caused Dane to explode, then she'd simply have to sit back and watch the fireworks. It was time he faced reality...someone needed to tell him to discard the hair shirt he'd been wearing for far too long.

"And I know you think you failed Helen and Angel," she continued. "But that was an accident. Just like Randy wrecking my car was an accident. No one could have foreseen it. No one."

She didn't know what had gotten into her. All she knew was that she felt utterly compelled to be completely and totally honest with Dane.

"I know you've set this course for yourself," she said. "This plan you have of remaining free and... what did you call it? Unencumbered. But I believe that all you're doing is hiding. Sheltering ourselves from life is impossible, Dane. You might think you're in control with all your careful choices and plans. But in reality, all you're doing is hiding."

Abruptly, Dane stood, taking her elbow and forcing her to her feet. He looked at Alva. "This is getting a bit personal. Excuse us while we find a little privacy."

Lacy had no recourse but to follow where she was being led. She looked back at Alva and had to suppress a smile when the elderly man was grinning like a monkey with an armful of bananas and giving her the thumb's-up sign of support.

Twilight had painted swipes of purple and pale pink across the sky, and Lacy knew that any other time, she'd have found the sight calming. But not now. There was too much left that needed to be said.

"What the hell do you mean?" Dane said when he finally stopped outside the brick building and turned to face her. "I'm *hiding?* I've never hidden from anything."

Disagreeing with him would only make him more angry.

"Look," she said, "all I know is that I've never known anyone who carries around as much baggage as you. And you're holding on to all of it with a white-knuckled grip."

She sighed. "It's not like you're alone. The past affects us all. I know I've been affected by mine. And you helped me see that. You were right. When you said my outrageous opinions were meant to scare men off. I've been protecting my heart. I have been. And I am grateful that you pointed it out."

Hitching the handle of her purse higher on her shoulder, she continued, "But now it's time for you to understand that some of the things you're feeling guilty over…weren't your fault at all." She shifted her weight. "You didn't choose for your mom to leave. You didn't choose for your father to get sick. And you sure didn't choose to lose your wife and daughter. But you are choosing to shut yourself off from happiness. From love. From *living*. By sticking to that well-thought-out plan, you think you're keeping yourself, and those around you, safe. But sometimes, Dane, when you make what you think is a safe choice, all you're doing is missing out on the gift— the awesome blessing—that fate has in store for you."

He didn't know what to say to her. Everything she

said made such logical sense. Why was he so damn determined to hold on to all these bad feelings?

As if she'd actually heard his unspoken query, Lacy whispered, "It's time to let go. Just let go of it all. And when you do, you're going to be so light and free that you'll feel as if you're floating. I promise you."

She heaved a sigh. "I'm not asking you to live in some fantasy. This world is real. And it's hard. Bad things are bound to happen. They happen every day. But you can't worry about them. You'll deal with things as they come. Someone who cares about you will be there for you."

Her blue eyes grew so intense that their color actually seemed to deepen.

Haltingly, she said, "I'll be that someone…if you'll let me."

No! He didn't want her to say any more. Offer any more.

He'd let himself think about being with her. He'd let himself dream. Imagine what life would be like if they were a couple. And that had been a mistake.

Seeing Randy wreck Lacy's car, pulling the boy, bleeding and crying, from behind the wheel, had brought back horrible memories for Dane. Had churned up feelings of how he'd failed in the past. His father. His wife. His daughter. And with all those "well, ifs" he'd come up with in the waiting room, he really had been searching for some reason to blame himself for Randy's injuries. Condemn himself for once again failing. Give himself yet another reason for turning away from Lacy.

The dissent in his heart must have showed on his face, must have clued her in to his feelings.

She nodded, her lips pursing tightly. "That's fine," she said. "Deny your feelings if that's what you need to do. But you and I both know that when I leave here, I'll be taking your heart with me. Just as I'll be leaving my heart here with you. I can't remain silent about my feelings any longer. I love you, Dane. And I realized this week that I've loved you for a very long time. But if you're not willing to admit what's between us—this *love* that keeps poking and jabbing at us, then I have no other option than—"

Her blue eyes welled and his heart wrenched in his chest.

"—to walk away from you."

This woman was amazing. She'd come into his life, turned things upside down, destroyed all his safe and easy answers. She'd made him see that there was never just one way to look at a situation...there wasn't just one way to live your life. Thousands of choices and options were just waiting to be tried.

If a man was brave enough to experiment with new ways of thinking. If a man had someone by his side.

Not too long ago, Lacy had challenged him by asking him if he really did want to model himself after his father. Dane knew now that he didn't. He didn't want to be anything like his dad, in fact. And Lacy had made him see that. His father had had his chance to live his life. Dane shouldn't ever have been made to feel shamefaced about wanting to live his. He'd felt guilty about having his own hopes and dreams, about reaching out for them, achieving them, for too long now. It really was time to let that go.

But was he brave enough to meet all the challenges Lacy had placed before him? Could he let go of the past entirely? Let go of his grief? Take that first step into the unknown future?

His gut tightened with familiar emotion. Fear.

"Lacy..." He let the rest of his thought trail as he heard his voice sounding as dry and brittle as old paper. He cleared his throat and tried again. "Lacy, you understand me better than anyone ever has."

Hope flickered in her sapphire eyes.

"But I need you to know...I'm scared."

Sympathy softened her beautiful features, but she remained utterly still. It was clear to him this was a choice she was forcing him to make. Whether he wanted her to stay or go, she would live with his decision. That much was apparent.

Since she'd barreled into his existence, she'd tried to teach him that life was rarely black and white. And lately the million shades of gray he'd experienced had left him feeling confused. But the idea of living without her would take away the brilliant kaleidoscope of color she'd brought to his days. He couldn't imagine an existence without her vibrancy. Couldn't survive without the radiant hues her love had painted on his black-and-white world.

"Will you help me?" he asked. "My wheels have been spinning in some deep ruts. Help me steer out of them." He reached out to her then, opening his arms wide.

And she raced into his embrace, the passionate kiss she planted on his lips silently but clearly conveying her answer.

Epilogue

Lacy was exhausted. And she feared she looked a wreck.

"You're beautiful," Dane said, bending over the hospital bed, lifting her hand to his lips and placing a kiss on the soft, sensitive skin of her inner wrist.

She smiled. He always knew just what to say, just what to do. "You lie so well."

"I'm not lying. The mother of my son is stunning."

This time she chuckled.

"You feeling up to some company?" Dane reached down into the hospital bassinet and scooped the baby up into his arms.

"Sure," Lacy told him. "Who's here?"

Before Dane could answer, Alva came into the room, waving a bouquet of flowers, kissing her cheek. "Hey, there," he said, concern tightening his voice. "How are you feeling?"

"Fine, fine," Lacy answered.

She waved a cheery hello to Belinda. She and Alva had married just a few short months after Dane and Lacy. The woman still beamed like a newlywed.

"Mom!" Lacy couldn't hide her surprise when her mother walked into the room.

"You don't think my daughter's going to have a baby without me being nearby, do you?"

Lacy basked in her mother's warm embrace. Movement at the door had her gasping.

"Randy! Get in here and give me a hug."

The teen had blossomed into quite a young man under Alva and Dane's friendship. His parents still stayed away a good bit, but as the boy had once told her, if a person doesn't have family around, friends can go a long way to fill the void.

Randy flushed beet red and his hug was quick, but it was apparent that he was pleased to be included in this visitation.

"Gimme that boy," Alva said to Dane, "before the nurse comes in and scoots us all out of here." Everyone sighed when the baby cooed and blinked.

"What's his name?" Lacy's mother asked.

"Gabriel," Dane told her. Then he looked at Alva, who supplied an approving smile.

"Angel would have loved being a big sister."

Dane nodded silently, moving over next to Lacy, taking her hand in his.

This baby was a symbol, she realized. Of hope. Of a second chance at fatherhood for Dane. Of the realization of a dream for herself. But most of all, baby Gabe was a representation of the love shared between Dane and Lacy. A love that had begun when the two of them were so young. A love that had endured twenty years of separation. A love that had freed their hearts and finally brought them together again.

"I believe this is the happiest day of my life," she told everyone in the room.

Clearly, her beloved husband was feeling too emotional to speak, so he simply held her close, and kissed her lips.

*   *   *   *   *

Modern Romance™
...seduction and
passion guaranteed

Tender Romance™
...love affairs that
last a lifetime

Sensual Romance™
...sassy, sexy and
seductive

Blaze™
...sultry days and
steamy nights

Medical Romance™
...medical drama on
the pulse

Historical Romance™
...rich, vivid and
passionate

MILLS & BOON®

Winner at

2001 IDEA INTERNATIONAL
DESIGN
EFFECTIVENESS
AWARDS

MAT5

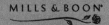

MILLS & BOON®

Tender Romance™

HIS MAJESTY'S MARRIAGE – Two exciting novellas!

The Prince's Choice by Rebecca Winters

Raoul Mertier has been betrothed to a stranger since he was born. But as his arranged marriage approaches he falls for another woman, Lee Gresham, and she doesn't have a drop of royal blood...

The King's Bride by Lucy Gordon

After one kiss Lizzie Booth senses that underneath King Daniel's cool, aloof exterior lies a passionate man, who despite his sense of duty *and* his best intentions is falling hopelessly in love...

THE CORPORATE BRIDEGROOM by Liz Fielding

Romana Claibourne must spend every working minute with her business rival Niall Farraday Macauley. Then – bang! – she's fallen in love – with her enemy!

THE TYCOON'S TEMPTATION by Renee Roszel

Powerful millionaire Mitchell Rath wants to take over Elaine Stuben's business. Mitchell has no time for emotional involvement but Elaine is seriously tempting this tycoon from his bachelorhood!

THEIR DOORSTEP BABY by Barbara Hannay

After years of trying for a baby, Claire and Alan Townsend are overjoyed to find a baby on their doorstep... But they must find out who his parents are before they claim him as their own...

On sale 3rd May 2002

Available at most branches of WH Smith,
Tesco, Martins, Borders, Eason, Sainsbury's
and most good paperback bookshops.

0402/02

0702/73/MB38

Coming in July

❦

The Ultimate Betty Neels Collection

❦

❋ A stunning 12 book collection beautifully packaged for you to collect each month from bestselling author Betty Neels.

❋ Loved by millions of women around the world, this collection of heartwarming stories will be a joy to treasure forever.

Available at most branches of WH Smith, Tesco, Martins, Borders, Eason, Sainsbury's and most good paperback bookshops.

GIVE US YOUR THOUGHTS

Mills & Boon® want to give you the best possible read, so we have put together this short questionnaire to understand exactly what you enjoy reading.

Please tick the box that corresponds to how appealing you find each of the following storylines.

32 Richmond Square

They're fab, fashionable – and for rent. When the apartments in this central London location are let, the occupants find amazing things happen to their love lives. The mysterious landlord always makes sure that there's a happy ending for everyone who comes to live at number 32.

How much do you like this storyline?

❑ Strongly like   ❑ Like   ❑ Neutral – neither like nor dislike
❑ Dislike   ❑ Strongly dislike

Please give reasons for your preference:

_____

_____

The Marriage Broker

This city agency matches marriage partners for practical as well as emotional reasons. Upmarket, discreet and with an international clientele, The Marriage Broker offers a personal service to match clients' needs and situations.

How much do you like this storyline?

❑ Strongly like   ❑ Like   ❑ Neutral – neither like nor dislike
❑ Dislike   ❑ Strongly dislike

Please give reasons for your preference:

_____

_____

A Town Down Under

Meet the men of Paradise Creek, an Australian outback township, where temperatures and passions run high. These guys are rich, rugged and ripe for romance – because Paradise Creek needs eligible young women!

How much do you like this storyline?

❏   Strongly like   ❏   Like   ❏   Neutral – neither like nor dislike
❏   Dislike   ❏   Strongly dislike

Please give reasons for your preference:

_____

_____

The Marriage Treatment

Welcome to Byblis, an exclusive spa resort in the beautiful English countryside. None of the guests have ever found the one person who would make their private lives complete…until the legend of Byblis works its magic – and marriage proves to be the ultimate treatment!

How much do you like this storyline?

❏   Strongly like   ❏   Like   ❏   Neutral – neither like nor dislike
❏   Dislike   ❏   Strongly dislike

Please give reasons for your preference:

_____

_____

Name: _____

Address: _____

_____

Postcode: _____

Thank you for your help. Please return this to:

Mills & Boon (Publishers) Ltd
FREEPOST SEA 12282
RICHMOND, TW9 1BR

NO STAMP NEEDED – postage has been paid.

MIRANDA LEE

Secrets & Sins *revealed*

SEDUCED BY HER BODYGUARD AND STALKED BY A STRANGER...

Available from 15th March 2002

books and a surprise gift!

We would like to take this opportunity to thank you for reading this Mills & Boon® book by offering you the chance to take TWO more specially selected titles from the Tender Romance™ series absolutely FREE! We're also making this offer to introduce you to the benefits of the Reader Service™—

★ FREE home delivery
★ FREE gifts and competitions
★ FREE monthly Newsletter
★ Exclusive Reader Service discount
★ Books available before they're in the shops

Accepting these FREE books and gift places you under no obligation to buy, you may cancel at any time, even after receiving your free shipment. Simply complete your details below and return the entire page to the address below. *You don't even need a stamp!*

YES! Please send me 2 free Tender Romance books and a surprise gift. I understand that unless you hear from me, I will receive 4 superb new titles every month for just £2.55 each, postage and packing free. I am under no obligation to purchase any books and may cancel my subscription at any time. The free books and gift will be mine to keep in any case.

N2ZEA

Ms/Mrs/Miss/Mr ....Initials...............................
BLOCK CAPITALS PLEASE

Surname ....

Address ....

....

....Postcode...............................

Send this whole page to:
UK: FREEPOST CN81, Croydon, CR9 3WZ
EIRE: PO Box 4546, Kilcock, County Kildare (stamp required)